## 'Fatherhood i of your priorit

He ignored the jibe. if you honestly thi spend my life wandering around knowing I have a child and having nothing to do with its life, then you really haven't the faintest idea of the kind of person I am.'

**Trish Wylie** resides in the border counties between the North and South of Ireland, splitting her not-long-enough days between her horses and writing. She started writing in primary school and dreamt about writing for Mills & Boon® from the moment she first read one in her early teens. She admits that it's important she's a little in love with her heroes. That way she can write what her heroine is feeling with more conviction and keep alive the hope that her own Mr Right might still be out there!

**Recent titles by the same author:**

HER REAL-LIFE HERO *(Jack and Tara's story)*
THE BRIDAL BET

# HER
# UNEXPECTED BABY

BY
TRISH WYLIE

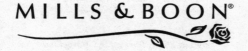

MILLS & BOON®

For the 'Newbies'.
My special friends: Ally, Hannah, Nic & Ola.

*First published in Great Britain 2004*
*Paperback edition 2005*
*Harlequin Mills & Boon Limited,*
*Eton House, 18-24 Paradise Road, Richmond, Surrey TW9 1SR*

© Trish Wylie 2004

ISBN 0 263 84216 9

*Set in Times Roman 10½ on 12 pt.*
*02-0205-48260*

*Printed and bound in Spain*
*by Litografía Rosés, S.A., Barcelona*

# PROLOGUE

THERE was something about a wedding that made families pick on the unattached members of their clan. When Dana Taylor's brother Jack finally met his match and tied the knot, the entire Lewis family, at least the female members, seemed to descend on Dana like flies round—well, honey.

Dana refused point-blank to liken herself to anything else that flies might hover around.

'You need to get back out there.'

'Out there *where*, exactly?' She kept a smile on her face, despite the fact she knew exactly what her eldest sister was referring to. Oh, yeah, she knew rightly. And *so* did not want to talk about it.

Tess sighed. 'Dating.'

'Oh, *that* out there.'

The next sibling in order of birth nodded as she took a sip of champagne. 'Honey, it's long since due. You can't just sit in that run-down house of yours and wait for the menopause to arrive.'

She couldn't? Why was she paying a mortgage, then, if it wasn't so she could have her own space to do whatever the hell she liked in? Dana blinked slowly, then narrowed her eyes as she thought.

Tess nodded in agreement with Rachel. 'Just because things didn't work the first time it doesn't mean there isn't someone else out there who'd be great for you.'

'You make it sound as if I live like some kind of hermit.'

'Don't you?' Rachel raised an elegant eyebrow. 'When's the last time you went out and had fun?'

'I took Jess to the beach last month.'

'That's mother-daughter fun. I mean…' She leaned her head in closer and winked. *'Fun.'*

'She means sex.' Her sister Lauren stated the obvious with a small nod.

Dana took a deep breath and leaned back in her chair. 'Why can't I just live alone and be happy?'

Tess snorted. 'Because you're not happy.'

'Who says I'm not?' she demanded.

'It's obvious you're not.'

'How the hell is it obvious?'

'See? If you were happy you wouldn't need to be defensive.'

Dana shook her head. 'Sometimes I really wish you wouldn't take the mothering role so seriously with us all. I'm fine.'

Tess, who had taken on the job of parent when their real mother had left them early on, simply shrugged her shoulders. 'You can say that to yourself as many times as you like, but you're lacking something in your life and we all know it. You do too, deep down. And I'm just saying that living every single day without ever taking any chances makes for a pretty empty life.'

'My life isn't empty. I have a daughter.' She glanced around the room until her blue eyes fell on the figure of her ten-year-old, currently attired as a flower girl. Her baby. The reason she got up in the mornings and worked until night. She was a mother, and there was simply no more rewarding job on the planet. 'I don't need another failed marriage to my name. We do just fine on our own.'

Rachel reached across to pat her hand, where it lay on the table. 'Hon, nobody is saying you should go looking for another husband. But maybe it wouldn't do any harm to find someone to spend some—' she smiled '—*quality time* with, every now and again.'

Dana blinked at her words. It wasn't that she didn't still believe in love or romance or passion. She just believed in them for other people, that was all. The Dana who had wanted those things for herself had long since received too many kicks in the teeth from reality.

'Are you suggesting I should just go out there and sleep with someone?' She tilted her head at her sisters. 'Just for the sake of it?'

There was a murmur of conflicting answers from around the small table. It was Tess who eventually gave the official viewpoint, just as she had in debates of old. 'A fling might do you good. You need to *feel* something again. You've switched yourself off, and that worries us all. It's just such a waste.'

Rachel nodded in agreement. 'It is. Dana, you're a beautiful, smart, determined, funny woman—but right now you're not letting yourself be any of those things. You shouldn't shut yourself away. Try having a little fun time for *you*. Have an affair, if that's all you want, but feel again. Feel what it's like to be a woman.'

Dana ignored the list of her attributes. After all, anything coming from a family member was bound to be biased, right? She opened her mouth to speak, then closed it for a moment to mull over the words.

She didn't think that she'd shut herself off. Okay, maybe at first, after the divorce, when everything had still smarted. When she'd had to sit down and admit she'd got married for all the wrong reasons. Maybe then she'd taken some time to re-evaluate her life and decided she was better alone for a while.

But, yes, perhaps it had been a *long* while.

'You lot aren't going to produce a queue of supposedly eligible men for me to test out, are you?' The thought made her skin crawl. The words 'charity dates' jumped unbidden into her head.

'No.' Lauren smiled at the thought, knowing fine well that her smile probably gave away the fact that it had been discussed at some point. 'We just think you should be more open to the idea of being Dana—*you*, not just the working mum—for a night or two here and there. When there's an opportunity to get lost for a moment, and it feels right, we think you should go with the flow.'

Tess interjected. 'We're not saying cruise the bars for men.'

'No, we're not saying that.' Rachel laughed at the very idea. 'As if you would. Just open yourself to the possibilities again, is all.'

'Let someone into your life.'

Dana sighed and looked to the balloon-strewn ceiling for intervention of some kind. They meant well. But it just wasn't in her to be some lust-ruled female who could jump into a short-lived affair. Maybe once upon a time, when she'd been young and wild and free. But that had got her married and pregnant and divorced.

When she looked back, the three familiar, similar faces were smiling encouragingly at her. She sighed as she shook her head. 'I'll try being more open to the idea of seeing someone if the opportunity presents itself, but I can't say that I'm ready to jump into some torrid affair— no matter how long it lasts or where it may take me.'

'One step at a time is fine.'

'We can live with that.'

'We just worry, you know.'

She knew they did. They were all happily settled now. Even their brother Jack had managed to get past his hang-ups and had opened himself to the woman who'd turned out to be his perfect mate. It made a cynic like Dana harbour the tiniest flicker of hope inside that all that happily-ever-after stuff could still exist somewhere.

And probably it did. It just really hadn't turned out to be for her. She'd had her chance and it hadn't worked. Now she had to just get on with it and live the life she had.

But she *was* making changes in her career, and working towards a better home for her daughter and herself. She had hopes and dreams for her daughter's life. She hadn't managed the wife part, but she could be the kind of mother her own hadn't managed to be.

Yes, indeed. Dana thought she was doing okay. *Just* okay, maybe, but that was enough for her. No matter what her sisters might think.

Mind you, that wasn't to say that it wouldn't be nice to be made to feel like a woman again for a while. That deep-down sensual woman who was hidden inside every female. *Mmm.*

Dana unconsciously ran her tongue across her mouth. It was just a shame that the kind of men who could bring that out in a female weren't hanging around all over the place. Though maybe that was just as well for the sake of survival.

Unconsciously her eyes moved across the room to the tall man who stood beside her brother. Adam, his best man. He was exactly the type she'd have looked at once upon a time. Tall, handsome, charm by the bucket. But she'd married one of those, and look where that had got her.

She sighed. When it came to passionate affairs Dana was in the middle of a huge desert—and it was a long,

*long* way to the next drink of water. No matter what her most basic needs might be.

No, passionate affairs just didn't land in her lap every day. But if one did? She smiled. Maybe just once wouldn't be so awful. After all, what harm could it do to feel again?

# CHAPTER ONE

*Six months later*

ADAM DONOVAN had the most amazing effect on women.

It was a gift, really, and probably had more to do with the way he looked than anything else. Though he could be charming when he really wanted to.

Dana watched as he managed to charm the pants off yet another customer.

It was truly disgusting.

She shook her head the tiniest amount. What on earth did all those women *see* in him? She decided to make an inventory of all things good about him. Though that did mean putting to the back of her mind the list she'd already formed of all things bad.

She'd worked with him for months now, and that latter list was getting long…

Okay, so there was his height. That was good. A woman always found it distracting if the man was so short that every conversation was directed at her breasts.

He was fairly broad too, indicating—incorrectly—that he spent a lot of time doing physical exercise to keep in shape. Dana, however, knew better. His idea of physical activity was probably limited to one particular room of the house, and that room wasn't the kitchen.

Oops. That was from the *All Things Bad* list, wasn't it?

He was a fairly good judge of clothes too. All the right clothes for all the right occasions. What he spent on a shirt would keep Dana and her daughter in groceries for

11

a week. On this occasion he was wearing a rather nice green one, which managed to highlight the colour of his eyes. Clever guy.

His face was fit for the pages of a glossy magazine on any newsagent's stand worldwide, complete with dimples, unbelievably white even teeth, that Dana was convinced in her own mind he had polished regularly, and a smile that could charm Eskimos into buying snow. Which, granted, was a terrific asset when it came to selling houses to people. Especially houses that didn't exist yet beyond a great big muddy hole in the ground.

Boyish dark blond hair, cut to just above his collar, with a side parting that managed to allow thick locks to fall across his forehead when he leaned forward to talk to a woman. As if by accident? Dana smiled slightly to herself. Like hell.

He really did tick a lot of boxes on the *All Things Good* list. He was a partner in a thriving company, came from a good family, and was generally an all-round eligible bachelor. Very eligible. Women really, *really* liked Adam.

Dana, meanwhile, found him a right royal pain in the ass. But then, after all, she worked with him.

He glanced up at her from beneath thick lashes. When he found her looking at him, with just a faint smile on her lips, his eyes narrowed slightly before he glanced away. Dana knew that he wasn't used to her smiling at him that often.

They were just very different people, that was all. Nobody had ever said they had to like each other. Which was just as well, really. Dana had managed to avoid him for years, but, since she'd bought a half-share of the company she owned and ran with her brother Jack, she had seemed to spend every single day arguing with him about something. Or about nothing. Or about pretty much *anything*, for that matter. When it came to Adam Donovan, it seemed that Dana was the only woman in the country who didn't see him as God's gift.

And she liked it that way.

Adam really wished that she'd stop smiling at him. It was disconcerting. Dana didn't smile without reason. She wasn't a natural-born smiler. Well, not so he'd noticed since she'd started working with him.

There he was, switching on the patented Donovan charm to seal them another contract, and she was *smiling* at him. How was a man supposed to work under these conditions?

Even as he was smoothly convincing Mr and Mrs Lamont of the benefits of under-floor heating in their modern interior, Dana Taylor was plotting something. He could feel it.

His partner's sister, now his partner herself, was a devious woman.

Adam had met devious women in his time. Dated a few, avoided a few, run away very fast from a few. But this one...well, suffice it to say she was devious on a whole new level.

Dana just had a knack of getting people to do things when they really didn't want to. They'd walk in with an attitude of 'no way, uh-uh, not doing that', and leave blinking and wondering how'd they managed to change their minds without knowing that they were doing it. It was a gift when it came to awkward customers or building crews, but it was annoying as all hell for someone who shared an office with her.

He glanced across at her again. Still smiling right at him. He felt his palms begin to sweat. Any minute now she'd have him wearing a skirt, and he probably wouldn't notice until there was a draught.

He let the Lamonts look at the sketches of their dream home and excused himself for a moment.

In two long strides he was stood in front of her.

'Okay, *what*?' His low tone dictated a voice level for a private conversation. She just stared at him, a blank expression on her face. He hated it when she did that.

'Is something wrong?'

He frowned. 'You tell me.'

The smiling continued. 'Nope, you've lost me, I'm afraid.'

Given the opportunity, he would love to. 'You're smiling.'

'Am I?' She smiled even more. 'Is there a law against that?'

'You don't smile.'

'I most certainly do. See?' She tilted her head and smiled a big fake smile that showed her straight teeth.

'You don't smile *at me*.'

'Does that upset you?' She blinked innocently.

He practically growled at her, instead whispering through slightly gritted teeth, 'You could just come on over and do that thing you do to help sell this house.'

She shrugged, smiling over his shoulder at the Lamonts. 'Oh, you're doing just fine, from what I can see.'

He studied her through narrowed eyes for several long moments. She was just so completely and utterly irritating. Everything about her irritated him, from her beautiful, flawless, not-a-hair-out-of-place exterior to her highly organised way of doing things. She was what would have once been termed as 'unflappable', and that just really annoyed Adam.

Adam, who lived by the seat of his pants in a chaotic
ttle world of his own.

It had worked for him his whole life, and he had never
elt there was a single thing wrong with it. Until Little
Miss Perfect came along.

'Stop smiling at me, then.'

She raised her elegant eyebrows a barely visible notch
nd looked up at him with cool blue eyes. 'Well, if it's
nnoying you so much...'

Adam shook his head, cupped one large hand over her
elbow and pulled her up from her perched position on the
edge of the desk. 'Customers, Dana. The people who pay
our wages.' He leaned close to her ear. 'People we are
not having an argument in front of. So, whatever it is
you're doing—quit it.'

Dana gently extricated her elbow from the warm grasp
that tingled through to her skin, smoothed the front of her
jacket with her hands and then side-stepped to get past
Adam's bulk. Her calm smile remained throughout. She
had irritated him, and that was always worthwhile.

Mrs Lamont smiled as she approached. 'The house is
beautiful, Dana. You have just done some wonderful
things with the plans for the interior. I'm so glad Lucy
recommended you.'

Dana smiled a more genuine smile. Louise Lamont's
sister Lucy had been a friend from her college days, and
Donovan & Lewis had designed her new home for her
just a few months ago. 'I'm really glad you like it, Louise.
All we did was put what you'd described into a few pic-
tures, and it's every bit as beautiful as you knew it would
be.'

Ah. There it was. That *thing* she did.

Adam smiled. Louise Lamont hadn't had any more of
an idea of what she wanted in a house than she had of

how to perform major brain surgery. Every design magazine she'd bought had changed her mind, until the place
was pretty much bound to end up looking similar to
Santa's grotto. Then there was Dana, and suddenly Louise
had loved a mixture of modern clean lines and classic
design, just as if she'd wanted it all from the beginning
and it had been her idea and not Dana's. The woman
really did believe that the house had been all her idea and
that she was practically a design genius!

*Devious.*

Louise positively beamed. 'Lucy can't wait to see you
at the reunion. She says she's going to tell everyone that
they should see Donovan & Lewis if they want a house
done.'

Dana felt warmth tinge her cheeks. She avoided
Louise's direct gaze and glanced over her shoulder. 'I'm
not actually going to make it to the reunion, I'm afraid.
We're terribly busy at the moment.'

Adam's eyebrows raised. She was uncomfortable? That
got his interest.

'Oh, but you must, Dana. Everyone's expecting to see
you since that article you had done in *Ireland's Home &
Hearth*.' She practically drooled the name of the design
magazine. It had been obvious from day one that that was
where Louise would have liked to see a photo spread of
*her* new house. Nothing to do with family comfort or a
personal pleasure in her surroundings…

'Not this time.' Dana smiled sweetly. 'But I'm sure I'll
make the next one.'

Now, that was a lie. Adam didn't know how he knew,
but he knew. He'd just caught Dana Taylor lying about
something. Oh, this was good. It had to be something big,
and Adam really, *really* needed to know what it was. That

kind of information could prove worth a fortune on the open market. How to flap the unflappable...

'Well, we're not so busy we couldn't spare you for one evening, Dana.' He stepped into the fray with a wide smile. 'A reunion, is it? I just love those—don't you, Louise?'

Louise fluttered her eyelashes at him, blushing faintly at his use of her first name. Good God. Dana wanted badly to be sick.

She turned her head slightly towards Adam and gave him one of her best 'stay the hell out' smiles. He'd witnessed them several times, so it shouldn't take much for him to know it was time to stop.

'I love them, Adam.' The woman actually giggled like a ten-year-old. Dana knew that for a fact, due to the endless giggling of her own ten-year-old. Oh, come on! She glanced at Mr Lamont to see if he'd noticed. But they'd obviously hit that period in their marriage where he had developed selective deafness.

'You should go, Dana. I bet it would be fun.'

Under normal circumstances she'd have wiped the grin off his face with a swift, cutting remark that would in turn have led to a disagreement and stony silence in the office for a few hours. Instead she took a small breath and stared him straight in the eye. 'You know how seriously I take my work, Adam. I *really* don't have time to go.'

Adam had translated her smile to mean 'stay the hell out', and grinned even wider. This was great. Seriously. He'd pay good money for moments like this. He slung an arm around her slender shoulders, fitting her pretty much under his expensively scented armpit, and, giving her a squeeze, continued to flirt with Louise.

'She's just so dedicated, isn't she? But I think I'll manage to persuade her to go along, don't you?'

'Oh, I'm sure if anyone can it would be you. I'm sure you're very persuasive.'

*Ugh!* The very thought. Dana managed not to shudder.

'Not this year. Maybe next time.' She side-stepped out of Adam's grip and pointed at the plans in front of Mr Lamont. 'You'll see we've kept the staircase open to allow light to flood through to the dining room.'

Mr Lamont nodded and studied the plans again.

Adam wasn't so easily distracted. 'When did you say this thing was, Louise?'

'Oh, it's this weekend. It's not too late for Dana to go. She was so popular back in college. I think that's why Lucy said Jim took such an interest—' Louise's eyes burned into the back of Dana's head. 'Oh, Dana, I do hope that's not the reason why you're not going. Is Jim going to be there? Oh, my, that *could* be awkward, couldn't it?'

Adam's eyebrows shot upwards. 'Jim who?'

Dana's eyes locked with Mr Lamont's for a second before she smiled and turned back round. 'Jim Taylor. My ex.' She aimed the words at Adam with an icy stare. 'And, no, that's not the reason I'm not going, Louise,' she lied without losing her smile. 'I really am busy. After all, we wouldn't want your project falling behind schedule, would we?'

Louise looked terrified at the very idea. 'Oh goodness, no, we wouldn't! I've planned to have photographers there for Christmas—haven't I, Paul?'

Paul Lamont glanced in her direction. 'If you say so, pet, I'm sure you have.'

'Well, then.' Dana nodded coolly. 'We'd better get these final plans approved, hadn't we?'

She shot a sidelong threatening glare at Adam as she turned. She could see plainly how he wanted to continue enjoying her discomfort, and with a spark of her eyes she warned him to drop the subject. *Just try it and see what happens, bucko!*

Adam took the hint and dropped it.

Until about twenty seconds after the Lamonts had left...

'You're not going to this reunion because your ex-husband might be there?' He nodded with a sarcastic twist of his lips. 'That's mature.'

Dana folded the Lamonts' plans carefully and placed them back inside their manila folder. 'None of your business, is it?'

'Possibly not, but—'

'I think you'll find the conversation ended with "possibly not".' She turned and frowned over at him. 'Stay out of things that don't concern you, Adam. You'll live longer that way.'

'What are you so worried about? Are you afraid he'll find out you still love him or something?' He waded on in with his size thirteens. 'Is that it? Or maybe you don't want him to know that you've stayed single all this time?'

On her way to the filing cabinet, Dana stopped dead and swung round with flashing eyes. 'I am *not* still in love with him! And I've damn well had dates since I split with him. Not that that's any of your bloody business either!'

Adam actually rocked back slightly. Little Miss Perfect had a temper? Since when? His mind moved more slowly than usual, distracted suddenly from simple thought by how her flashing eyes and flushed cheeks changed her usual cool exterior. She looked *sexy*. All she needed was to do the whole 'remove one pin and shake her hair loose' thing...

He recovered with, 'You don't have a date, do you?'

She placed a hand on her hip, cocked her head to one side and practically spat the word at him. *'What?'*

'For this reunion. You don't have a date.' He folded his arms across his broad chest and took a deep breath. 'And you don't want to see him with some sweet young thing on his arm while you're doing the whole lonely-pint deal.'

Dana truly, *truly* hated him in that moment. If she hadn't before, she did now. There was nothing more smug than an already arrogant male being proved right.

'Whatever you think.' She turned and marched the last couple of steps to the filing cabinet, wrenching the drawer open with too much force when she got there. Damn him. She hated losing her temper.

There was silence for a few moments, as Adam thought and Dana started counting inwardly to calm her temper.

Adam took another breath. 'I'm right, then.'

'Oh, gee.' She turned and glared. 'Aren't you always?'

Adam recognised sarcasm. Even when it had all the grace of a hippo in high heels. Not that Dana was the teeniest bit over the recommended weight for her height. God forbid. That wouldn't be perfect, would it? No, the woman curved where she was supposed to curve, both in and out.

'Pretty much.'

Dana took a deep breath and moved around the office with silent grace, collecting files and errant pens and putting them back into their allotted places. 'Now that you've managed to score a hit, can we drop this one?'

*No chance.* Adam smiled inwardly. She should know him better by now.

'So why can't you get a date?'

'You tell me—you're the one with all the answers.'

'Have you tried—hell, I dunno—' he shrugged and leaned back against his desk '—*asking* someone?'

She actually laughed out loud. 'You know, I haven't.'

With a small turn of her patent leather heel she looked him straight in the eye, folding her arms across her chest and leaning back against her own desk in an exact mirror of his stance. 'Who would I ask, exactly?'

'You're bound to know someone.'

'With my schedule?'

'Well, you must have friends who know someone.'

She smiled mirthlessly. 'Not someone who'd be suitable for the whole—' she unfolded her arms to make speech marks in the air with her fingers '""—slap in the face, up yours, Jim" effect I'd want, no.' She folded her arms again.

Adam's eyes narrowed. 'You need someone to *irritate* him?' Her personality wasn't enough? 'What—someone to make him jealous or something?'

'Not in the way you think.'

He continued to stare at her. 'In what way, then?'

She took a deep breath and shook her head. 'You wouldn't understand, so what's the point?'

'Try me.'

It would be a new direction if she decided to take that path. It would mean telling him something private, something vaguely embarrassing—even a little, well, girlish in places. It would also be opening a small window into her life. Into the secrets and pain she carried with her, well buried, from her past. In giving him that information she would be giving him ammunition for their next argument. And, even if he didn't ever use it, she would still know he knew. It was a big risk.

He watched the debate unfold in her eyes as she continued staring at him. They were the only part of her that she wasn't able to mask with an air of remote coolness. When she was annoyed or irritated, amused or excited by something, it all showed in her eyes. It was why she wore sunglasses so often to hide them, or dropped her chin, or turned her head slightly. Oh, yeah, he knew those little tricks of hers—knew them well enough to know when he'd scored a hit.

'How about if I promise not to use it against you at a later date?'

She was surprised by the offer. It almost seemed sincere. Adam Donovan trying to be nice? Nah. Not in her lifetime.

'Why do you need to know?'

He shrugged again. 'Maybe I might actually be able to help.'

A small smile twitched at the edges of her mouth. 'Oh, really? How exactly would you see that working? And, more importantly, what would it cost me?'

'You have a very suspicious mind.'

'Around you? Yes, indeed I do.'

'I just offered you an olive branch of sorts.'

'Yes, you did, and that's why I'm suspicious.'

'Would it kill you to try trusting me just once?' He frowned at her. 'It's not like you've tried it before, is it?'

He had a point. Trusting him was something she'd never done or considered since she'd met him. And there probably was an underlying reason for that, if she decided she wanted to look for it. But then, in fairness, she'd seen him in action. Apart from his business dealings, Dana had witnessed nothing that would lead her into trusting him with personal information. If she'd become anything in the last eight years it was a survivalist. But she was curious nevertheless.

'Again: why do you want to know, exactly?'

Good question. Blinking at her questioning eyes, he decided not to search too deeply for a reason. He'd go with a sensible answer. He worded it carefully. 'Maybe if you actually took the time to trust me with information occasionally, I might do the same thing.'

'And that would be interesting to me because…?'

He pressed his lips together and managed to swallow a sarcastic answer. 'It might improve the atmosphere in this office, for one thing. If we tried actually getting to know each other a little instead of this constant bickering.'

She took his words and mulled them over in her head for a few moments. The bickering could be tiring sometimes; that much was true. Other times it could be quite stimulating…occasionally a little fun, she admitted reluctantly.

But could she manage to give a little without ending up giving away too much? That was the question. It was a big step in their 'relationship'. Maybe if she tried it the once, she could decide better what to do the next time…

Hell. Desperate times called for desperate measures.

She surprised them both with, 'Okay.'

His eyebrows raised slightly. That had been a tad too easy, hadn't it? He felt a need to look around for the catch. But he was a big guy. He'd play. 'So, what is it with you and this guy, then?'

Taking a deep breath, she waded in. 'I'm not prepared to let him get the better of me.'

'In what way?'

She knew she had to be tired to be even having this conversation, but she was in it now. She sighed. 'He has a new girlfriend.'

Adam waited patiently.

'And from all accounts I'm led to believe she's drop-dead gorgeous and highly successful at everything she does.' She gritted her teeth and forced the words out. 'I can't let him do the whole…'

He unfolded his arms to mimic her earlier statement. '"Slap in the face, up yours, Dana" thing?'

'Exactly.'

'So it's tit for tat?' He nodded wisely. 'I'm still going with my "That's mature" response.'

Dana stood up and walked round her desk to retrieve her overcoat. 'I knew you wouldn't understand.'

'Because there's more, and I damn well know it.' He blocked her way when she lifted her bag and tried to leave. 'So what is it?'

Blue eyes glared at his chest for a moment before eventually looking up. 'Since he walked out on Jess and me he's become Mister Successful—Mister Everything-He-Wasn't-When-He-Was-With-Us. And meanwhile, back at the ranch, I've just about managed to hold my head above water.'

From the emotion he saw in her eyes he knew she was being honest, and it affected him. His voice softened of its own accord. 'You've done okay.'

That was how much *he* knew. 'Yeah, sure—just okay. Nothing special, nothing amazing, nothing at all in my personal life. And I'll be damned if I'm going to turn up at that reunion and have everyone talking about how poor Dana has only just coped without good old Jim.'

He mulled her words over. Somehow he knew there was more to this story. And he wanted to know what it was. Maybe there was more to Dana Taylor than the whole Little Miss Perfect thing she did so damn well.

She didn't like him much. He knew that and was quite happy with it, in fact, because the feeling was mutual. But he could be a nice guy when he tried. And maybe, just maybe, if he tried being nice the one time she might be less of a nightmare to work with. She'd *owe* him, in fact. Adam liked that idea.

'Okay. *I'll* be your date.'

# CHAPTER TWO

'ADAM offered to be your date? *Really?*'

Dana blinked across at her sister-in-law. They'd become close incredibly fast, considering Dana's lack of trust for new people. But it hadn't taken long for her to see how much her brother Jack loved Tara, and within a short period of time it had become obvious why. She was special. If a tad...well, unusual at times.

At that precise moment they were curled up on the sofa in Jack and Tara's living room. Tara, nearly five months pregnant, was wearing a huge T-shirt with an arrow that pointed down to her stomach and the words 'Bun in the Oven' emblazoned across her chest.

'Yes, and my face must have looked exactly like yours does now when he said it.'

'What did you say?'

'I think I stood with my mouth open long enough to catch flies.'

'And then you said...?'

'I said he had to be kidding.'

'And he said?'

'That it was a genuine offer. And *Wouldn't it get me out of a hole?*' She mimicked his voice.

Tara grinned, her grey eyes wide. 'So you said...?'

'That in order for it to get me out of a hole it would have to be believable, and we weren't exactly a match made in heaven.'

Tara waved her finger in the air. 'You've got a point there.'

25

'I thought so,' Dana sighed. 'I mean, who on earth is going to watch the two of us together for more than sixty seconds and not recognise the fact that we can't stand each other? That man could make a nun commit murder.'

'You've mentioned that. Jack finds it hilarious.'

'He would.'

'Though you have to admit…' Tara looked thoughtful for a moment, then spoke over the rim of her cup. 'Adam definitely fills the requirements for an ''in your face, Jim'' date.'

'Possibly.' She'd already admitted that fact to herself on the drive over, although it had taken ten miles before she'd allowed the thought to take root. In fact, she'd done the whole 'pros and cons' list again, as it happened. If there was nothing else about Dana she was at least logical. She thought things over. Assessed them carefully. *Very* carefully.

Adam as a partner was just too ridiculous.

'Walking in on his arm certainly wouldn't do your reputation any harm.'

'Until he opened his mouth.'

Tara smiled as Dana sipped at her tea. It never ceased to amaze her, the differences between Jack and his sisters. Especially this one. Whereas Jack was a spontaneous, off-the-cuff guy, who followed his heart in everything he did, Dana was at the complete opposite end of the scale. Sometimes it was as if the very thought of losing control of anything around her was just too big a step for her to take.

Then, just every so often, there would be a tiny glimpse of her that matched her brother. But those glimpses were rare. Rare and a wonder to the beholder.

Dana really had no idea of her own worth as far as Tara could see.

'Aw, c'mon, Dana—he could charm the pants off the entire room within about twenty seconds of getting there, and you and I both know it. He's a man's man, as well as every woman's idea of a complete stud muffin.'

Dana mulled the words over for a moment and then sighed. 'But not the type who'd date a woman like me. It'd be completely and utterly unbelievable, and that's why it would never work.'

'*Why* wouldn't you be the type of woman he'd date?'

Dana's eyebrows rose slightly at the question. Then she shrugged. 'I'm not glamour model material. I'm more...hell, I don't know...the kind of woman that a bank manager would date.'

'You fancy your bank manager?'

That drew the required smile. 'You'd know the answer to that if you ever saw him. The only attractive thing about that man is the fact that he controls my overdraft.'

'And Adam?'

Dana turned in her seat to stare at Tara. 'You think I find anything attractive about Adam Donovan?'

'You're not blind.'

'He doesn't look like the back of a bus. I'll give you that.'

'And?'

'And?' Dana's eyes widened. She wasn't about to make any confession on the subject of whether or not she found Adam remotely attractive. Tara would just have to go fishing in another pond. 'There isn't an *and*, Tara. Other people may think he's the be-all and end-all, but I know him. I work with him every day and I think he's an arrogant—'

'Yes, I know, I know.' Tara waved her hand. There was just no arguing on the subject of Adam with Dana. And the romantic side of Tara had tried. 'I get that. But you have to admit that he would be one hell of a candidate for the reunion. You'd just need to try and forget all you know about him for one little evening and then you could go back to normal. Sounds fairly simple.'

Dana blinked as she thought, the conflict visible in her expressive eyes.

Tara continued, 'By *not* being there, in a way you'll have let Jim win, don't you think?'

'How will I?'

'He'll think you didn't go because you knew he'd be there with Melanie. He'll think it matters to you that he's with someone and you're not.'

Yes, he damn well would. But it was Adam Donovan they were talking about, here. Adam bloody Donovan.

Dana searched for another exit route. 'I wouldn't be believable as someone Adam Donovan would look twice at.'

'Because you're not his type?'

'Exactly. Like I said.'

Tara shook her head. Didn't Dana ever look in the mirror? 'I think I need that explained better.'

With a frown, Dana looked away from Tara's probing gaze. 'He exclusively dates the glamour girl type—all make-up and shiny hair and cleavage. The vaguely vacant type is all I've ever seen come by for lunch. Trust me. I'm not like that.'

Tara studied Dana's controlled exterior. To all the world she was sleek, elegant, sophisticated. Nothing was ruffled or out of place, from the top of her head to the tips of her toes. Everything indicated that she was matter-of-fact, ultra-smart and businesslike, reliable. Nothing about her exterior indicated her creative personality or the wicked sense of humour that every member of her family possessed.

Tara's eyes wandered over the dark hair swept back into a neat chignon at the neck of her jacket, the face with delicate features barely touched by make-up. *Ah-ha*...

'We could do a makeover.'

'A what?'

'A makeover. Recreate Dana Taylor for one night.' Tara's smile grew, her imagination kicking in. 'That'd get the room talking. The brand-new, sexy Dana with the drop-dead gorgeous Adam Donovan. Hell, that's bound to make you the talk of the town for a few months. "In your face" material if ever I heard it.'

Dana watched as the idea formed in her sister-in-law's eyes, her face now animated. This thing was getting out of control. Really. It was a runaway train.

'What *kind* of makeover?'

'You just had to volunteer didn't you?'

Adam looked at his own eyes in the rearview mirror.

'Yeah, and you nearly, *almost* got away with it. But, no. You went and volunteered, and now you're going to a reunion with the woman you spend half your life trying to get away from.' He raised an eyebrow. 'You're a genius, aren't you?'

With practised ease he honed his sports car round a corner at its usual sixty miles an hour, and then swore as he had to reduce speed rapidly to make the turn into Jack and Tara's lane way.

His business partner and best friend had let the bachelor team down badly when he'd gone and got married. But Adam had forgiven him—just about. After all, the man was happy—hell, contented, almost. He could forgive the act if it had that result on a guy he loved like a brother. But as for Jack lumbering Adam with his pain-in-the-ass sister... Well, that would take longer to forgive.

He parked his favourite toy, took a deep breath, and walked up the steps and onto the porch of the huge Victorian house. The door swung open before he got to it.

'Hey, pal.' Jack Lewis grinned at him from the doorway. 'Nice tux. Don't you look sweet?'

'Anyone ever told you how much you'd suit a black eye?'

'Nope, but if you reckon you're man enough to try it out...'

Adam grinned across at him. The two men were of equal height at the six-two mark. 'Nah, wouldn't dare. Your wife would kick my ass.'

'Indeed she would.' Jack stood back to allow Adam to step into the hallway, his hand immediately reaching across to slap his back. 'This is a nice thing you're doing, by the way, so I'll just get this out of the way right now...' He waited until Adam looked him in the eye. 'I appreciate it.'

He damn well should. Adam smiled at the younger man. 'No problem.'

Jack's face changed slightly. 'If you knew what that useless ex-husband of hers—'

Adam had moved closer as Jack began to confide in him, but was distracted when movement caught the corner of his eye from the top of the stairs. Turning his head, he glanced upwards as Dana approached.

If his mind hadn't recognised the woman as Dana Taylor he'd have fallen in love there and then. She was, quite simply, stunning.

'Are you going to keep on looking at me like that all night?' She didn't look across at him as he smoothly changed gears and sped along the wide road.

Adam gritted his teeth. This was going to be the longest night of his life. 'And how exactly *am* I looking at you?'

She took a breath and stared at the alien that was her own reflection in the windscreen. 'Like you're a chocaholic and I'm a bar of best Swiss.'

He glanced at her from the corner of his eye. How in God's name had she noticed that, when she'd spent the last twenty minutes staring straight ahead? The atmosphere in his small car couldn't have been cut in half with a chainsaw.

'That's how most men with a pulse look at women who wear dresses like you're wearing—didn't you know?' He smiled sarcastically. 'It's a chemical reaction, so don't get your G-string in a twist.'

Dana sincerely hoped his remark was flippant and not because he could actually see what she was wearing beneath the dress.

Tara had been like a woman possessed from the moment the word *makeover* had left her lips. Dana, left to herself, would never have worn a dress like this in a billion years. After all, at her age she had things like hypothermia to consider.

'Well, could you kindly stop it?'

'Why? Aren't I supposed to be your date? Let me tell you, if this was a real date and you wore that dress we wouldn't even have left the house yet—and you'd have your make-up to fix in about an hour.'

She squirmed slightly on her seat, his words conjuring images in her mind that her imagination had no business creating. For the entire day she had been trying to think up ways of getting out of this charade. But Tara had been having so much fun with it all, and in a small way it *was* flattering to have people stunned by her transformation.

Even if the majority of them were family and the other was the one person on the planet who irritated her most.

'Well, we'll never know, will we? Because this *isn't* a real date.'

They drove on in silence for several long minutes, each of them alone with their thoughts. Adam caught her squirming again in the seat beside him and smiled with sudden realisation. 'You're uncomfortable as hell with how you look tonight, aren't you?'

Great. Insight. When had he developed that?

'I'm not exactly dressed as me tonight, am I?' The words spilled out. She really shouldn't have drunk all that red wine while Tara got her ready.

He shrugged. 'Not as the anally retentive you that I work with every day, no.'

'Anally retentive?' She turned her head to frown at his words. 'You think I'm anally retentive?'

Adam glanced at her and grinned. 'Hell, yes. You think you aren't?'

Was she? She mulled his words over in her mind as the car sped towards their destination. The Dana of old would never have been described as anally retentive. Far from it. She'd been wild back in the day—a practical joker, a live wire. But back then she'd been carefree. Life had changed that. Now she was a single mother, and responsibility came with that title.

Maybe she *was* a tad anally retentive in her working life—when Adam saw her. It was the only part of her life she'd ever allowed him to see. She'd been careful about that. Even Jess, her daughter, had never been brought to the office. So he really had nothing else to base his assumption on, did he? She shouldn't actually have cared that he thought it. But somehow she did. It ruffled her feathers.

'I like things at work to be organised.' She tilted her head slightly as she said the words in a sharp tone. 'And you can't tell me that that office didn't need some organisation. You couldn't even find a pen when I first arrived.'

It was true. But that hadn't stopped the business from being successful. They'd always got the important things done on time. It might have meant a night or two of burning the midnight oil to get there. But they'd always managed it. Just.

He wasn't so pig-headed that he wouldn't admit that her need for neatness and systems had helped. Now the place ran like a well-oiled machine. But in a small way that had taken some of the fun out of it for Adam.

'You could loosen up a bit and it wouldn't kill you.'

'I'm loose.' She blushed at her own words and he grinned across at her.

'I don't need to know about your personal life, Dana.'

'You don't know anything about me!'

Not beyond what she wanted him to see. He knew that much. Had known it for months. It wasn't as if he hadn't known Jack's sisters before, but Dana was as much a mystery to him now as she'd been when he'd first set eyes on her. Elusive, almost. It was another one of the many things that bugged him about her.

'You're right. I don't.' He focused his gaze back on the road as they approached the turning to the hotel where the reunion was being held. 'Any more than you know anything about me. But that doesn't stop you from judging me, does it?'

She snorted quietly. 'And you're going to tell me you have some hidden side to you, are you? It's well hidden, isn't it?'

He screeched to a halt in front of the large building, yanking the handbrake with superfluous force before silencing the purr of the engine and turning to scowl across at her.

'You don't *want* to get to know me, Dana. That's your problem. You're so bloody uptight that you prefer to just place people in safe little boxes and never look any deeper than what you see on the surface. Makes everything very safe and secure for you, doesn't it?'

Her heart beat a little faster as her anger grew. 'And this is precisely the reason I didn't want to bring you to this damned reunion. We're not even inside the building and already we're having an argument!'

Adam took a deep breath and looked out of the windscreen. He watched several people in evening dress filtering in through the hotel's glass doors. They were here now. And, as much as he wanted to turn the car around and take her right back to where they'd come from, he was a bigger man than that. He wouldn't let her off that easily. She was just so determined to be right all the damned time. Well, not this time. He'd make the evening convincing if it killed him.

'You need to pretend you like me for this to work.'

'I'd win an Oscar for that.'

He turned to look at her again. 'Give it a try. Pretend I'm someone else, if you like. Because that's what I intend doing with you.'

'*Pretend* I like you?'

He nodded. 'Yes.'

'Forget who you are?'

'Yes.' His jaw clenched. 'Just for a few hours. Try looking at me as a man, and not as something you picked up on the heel of your boot. I can do it if you can.' Though it would take some effort. 'All we have to do is forget about real life for tonight. Make like we're two people who just met and are still getting to know each other. No preconceptions, no false judgements. Live for the moment and all that.'

He made it sound so simple. She blinked across at him. Was it? Was it just that simple? Forget that he was Adam for one evening and get to know him as if he was just some guy? Like a blind date of sorts? She took a breath. It would be a stretch.

The old Dana would have pulled this off with her eyes shut. The old Dana would have found it all hilarious, a great joke—a challenge, even. Was there any of that girl left any more? Or had reality squashed her down too much?

Another deep breath. She would try. It was a college reunion, for crying out loud. If that couldn't remind her of the girl she'd used to be then what could? She was walking into that room completely made over, *à la* Cinderella. And with a ridiculously attractive Prince Charming type at her side, too. What the hell else did she need to pull it off?

Guts, possibly? She'd had those once.

'What's wrong, Dana?' His voice dropped to a deep, intimate note. 'No guts, no glory. If you're too chicken for this, or if you're not woman enough to walk into that room in that dress...you just say the word.'

Damn, damn, damn. Why did it have to be *him*?

It was as if the room went still when they walked in. To the outside view they made one hell of a couple.

Dana couldn't tell if the assembled company had actually done the whole silent thing, due to the band playing on stage at one end of the large area, but heads certainly turned and conversations were certainly interrupted.

Dana smiled. It was actually a nice feeling. She couldn't remember the last time people had looked at her as if—well, like they were doing right that second. With a sense of awe, almost. With maybe a touch of 'wow' in their expressions. It felt good.

Adam noticed her smile and smiled himself, moving his hand up to touch her back, to guide her into the room. He was reminding himself to play the game. He only remembered when his hand touched soft skin that her dress had no back.

His hand jumped away as if burned before he forced himself to set it back in place, moving his long fingers in an unconscious caress as he ushered her into the crowd. Her skin felt good, his mind recognised, silken and warm to the touch—and that was only on her back. Being male, his mind wandered to other areas where a woman's skin was softer still. If she was this soft where his hands were now...

He cleared his throat, suddenly noting how warm the room was for so early in the evening.

Dana had jumped too when his hand touched her. Surprise, she told herself. After all, it wasn't as if Adam made a habit of touching her naked skin on a daily basis. When his hand settled the second time, and those long fingers of his began their smooth caress, she felt her pulse beat erratically. She'd always known he had quite an effect on women. And she'd always wondered why. But if the simple touch of his hand had that kind of effect then she now had a pretty fair idea of the 'why'. TMI, as her daughter would say. Too much information.

She glanced up at him with a tilt of her head, her blue eyes exploring his profile for signs that he'd noticed her reaction. After a second he glanced down and their eyes locked. He moved his hand along her back again, his forefinger tracing a line along the ridges of her spine, downwards to the inward curve of the small of her back.

Her eyes grew heavy. He was good at this make-believe stuff.

Adam watched her reaction to his touch. She was quite the little actress. Pretend she was someone else. That was what he'd said he'd do, right? Well, hell, it wasn't going to be tough. The woman in front of him was a complete stranger—as far removed from the Dana he knew as…as Godzilla from Brigitte Bardot.

This woman was *hot*. Hot to the touch, hotter than hell to look at—and, had an alarm bell not sounded at the back of his head to remind him occasionally of who she was, Adam would have wanted her. Big style.

As she flicked the edge of her tongue across her mouth he leaned towards her ear. 'I think we got their attention.'

Waiting until he raised his head slightly, she looked into his eyes and smiled. 'I'd say so.'

His eyes wandered from hers to a lock of curled hair that brushed against her flushed cheek. He reached out to turn it between his fingers, his other hand still continuing its caress against her spine. 'So, do you want to mingle, get a drink, dance? Or maybe…' His eyes met hers again. 'Maybe we should just find a corner to continue convincing them in.'

If he did much more convincing Dana was fairly sure she'd explode. Her poor pulse would just beat its way right out of its little passageway. The nerves she'd had about attending the stupid reunion and all that red wine were obviously making her react in ways she wouldn't have under normal circumstances. Yeah, that was it. It was a form of stage fright, that was all. This acting thing was a toughie. But she wasn't going into any corner to convince anyone of anything when Adam was looking at her like that.

It was as if she'd stepped into a different reality. But

she could deal with it. She could make it through—somehow…

'I think I'd like a drink.'

His smile widened, awarding her a glimpse of those perfect white teeth and those dimples of his. 'I can arrange that.' He suddenly leaned down. Dana tilted her head at that exact moment to listen to what he was saying. The two movements in the same split second caused his lips to just barely touch across the sensitive skin below her ear, and his voice tickled against the goosebumps the touch had created. *'Chicken.'*

She watched him as he walked away from her, his broad shoulders stretching the material of his jacket as he moved. About six steps away he looked over his shoulder at her and winked. Dana laughed as he turned away again. He really did have enough arrogance to fill the room. Reluctantly she had to admit inwardly that it had a certain element of charm about it. Wild horses wouldn't drag the words from her lips, though.

Even as she laughed at his departing figure she was suddenly surrounded by arms, and lips kissing her cheeks. When she was finally freed she glanced round at the four grinning faces of her friends from the old days. The ones who had known the old Dana best.

'Oh, my lord, Dana, where did you get that hunk of man from?'

'How long have you been seeing him?'

It was Lucy who eventually stepped forward to silence them all.

'Now, girls, give Dana time to catch her breath.' She winked sideways at her. 'And after seeing you in action I'd say you *need* a moment or two to catch your breath.' She flapped a hand in front of her face before smiling a warm smile. 'I never knew you two were an item. I thought you just worked together.'

Tracey McKenna blinked at her. 'You know that man?'

'Of course I do.' Lucy nodded. 'He's Adam Donovan— as in Donovan & Lewis, the designers. Dana and Adam work together.'

'You work together? How do you concentrate long enough to get anything done?'

Dana smiled. 'Believe me, it's tough. But I manage somehow.'

'He's sex on a stick, isn't he?'

'God, you always could get them.' Ella Dawson blinked at her with a twinkle in her eye. 'If there was a great-looking guy within fifty paces he always ended up chasing round after you.'

Dana searched for a hint of sarcasm in the woman's eyes and blinked in surprise when she found none. She examined the words. *Really?* Ella thought *that*? She glanced around to see if a crowd of men had formed that she hadn't noticed. Nope.

'You really need to get glasses, Ella. There's no rush of men in my general direction.'

'Not while you have Adam Donovan with you, there's not!'

No, and pretty much never, actually. She was a single parent who was apparently anally retentive; surely that in itself was enough to keep the men from breaking down her front door?

Lucy smiled. 'You were always popular with the guys, Dana. And, in that dress, what warm-blooded male wouldn't be interested? You look sensational.'

'Doesn't she, though? I said pretty much the same thing.'

The deep, familiar voice sounded beside her left ear,

and Adam charmed all of the women as he rewarded them with a smile they each thought was meant only for them. He then handed Dana her glass with a sparkle in his eye, and immediately replaced his hand on her back, where the skin was still warm from the last time he'd touched her.

Dana raised an eyebrow as she sipped at her wine. He'd said no such thing, actually. What he'd done was gape at her from the bottom of the stairs, then steal glances at her on the trip over. And now he felt he had *carte blanche* to keep *touching* her.

'We were just saying how typical it is of her to end up with the best-looking guy in the room.' Tracey leaned towards Adam as she spoke. Lots of women did that, Dana knew.

Adam blinked. 'Really? Bit of a goer, was she?'

Dana gritted her teeth beneath a smile and elbowed him hard in the ribs. 'Isn't he just the funniest?'

'Just a small part of my many charms—isn't it, babes?'

And if he called her *babes* again she was going to elbow him lower next time. She felt him move his hand across her back to her hip, leaving his thumb to play against her skin as he pulled her closer to his side.

'She was just so much fun to be around.'

Adam gaped slightly at Lucy, the only one of the women he'd met before. Fun? To be around? Dana Taylor?

*'Really?'*

Dana glared up at him. If he was supposed to be pretending he was in some great relationship with her surely he shouldn't look so damned surprised at the thought that she might actually be fun?

Fortunately Lucy appeared to be a couple of wine glasses past observant. 'Oh, yeah! I can't tell you the number of times I've seen her dance on tables or lead us all on some madcap trip somewhere. Do you remember the Twenty-Four-Hour Club, Dana?'

As his thumb continued to move along the edge of the material of her dress, over her skin and what he thought might be the minute string of her underwear, Adam's mind worked overtime. He sincerely hoped that the Twenty-Four-Hour Club was no relation to the Mile-High Club, or he would never be able to share an office with Dana again.

Dana's face began to flame. Not so much because of Lucy's reminiscences of the past as the fact that she was now being completely distracted by Adam's hand against her. The last thing she needed was for him to find his earlier assumption as to the kind of underwear a woman was forced to wear beneath this type of dress had in fact been correct. She tried to squirm subtly further away from the steel wall of his body.

But Adam was having none of it. He pressed his hand firmer against her hip and drew her closer. With a downward glance that said *Oh, no you don't*, he asked the obvious question. 'Twenty-Four-Hour Club, babes?'

She swallowed. He really could be quite intense close up, couldn't he? She damped her lips. 'Probably not what you're thinking it was.'

'Then why don't you tell me?'

'It was basically an excuse for drunken trips away.'

Dana grimaced at Lucy's choice of words. They were accurate, which didn't help her cause any. She gulped down more wine.

Lucy, meanwhile, continued. 'The idea was to get as far away from base—which was college—as possible, and back again within twenty-four hours, on a pre-agreed budget.'

Adam smiled at the thought. 'To anywhere?'

'Oh, yes. We got all over the place—didn't we, Dana?'

Dana opened her mouth to answer, then closed it again as Lucy continued. 'It started with a boat trip to Scotland, then one to France, then some of us got a bit further afield until Dana the Master topped us all.'

His smile upgraded to a grin as he looked down at her. 'Where'd you end up?'

'New York.' She finally managed to get a word in edgewise.

'On a budget of what?'

Lucy laughed. 'That was the best bit. She dressed up as some kind of medical person, and carried a pig heart in a freezer case a medical student mate of hers had got from the hospital. She blagged her way onto the flight for virtually nothing because she was carrying a donor organ. Took some major flirting, from what I've heard, but she was famous after that.'

Adam looked at her with more respect than she'd ever seen before from him. Trust him to value her more for her immoral and irresponsible ways of old than for her 'anally retentive' organisation around the office. Typical.

'I'm impressed.'

'You just would be, wouldn't you?'

He tilted his head. 'I'm seeing a whole new side to you here.'

She managed a small smile at the truth in his words. 'I guess you are.'

His thumb moved slowly backwards and forwards against her skin. Hypnotic, almost. With a lazy blink of his green eyes he lowered his voice to a deep rumble. 'Anything else you want to tell me about?'

She hadn't wanted him knowing anything in the first place. The hypnotic movement continued against her skin. 'What do you want to know?'

His eyes looked deep into hers. *What changed you?* The question formed in his brain and almost made it to his mouth. But he closed it just in time. He needed to keep reminding himself this was Dana Taylor, his very own personal nemesis, the woman who made work days seem much longer than their allocated eight to twelve hours.

A voice sounded from outside the sexually charged bubble they were creating. 'You know she sings?'

# CHAPTER THREE

IT WAS officially becoming the longest night of her life.

*You know she sings?* had progressed as the evening continued to *You should sing with the band for old times' sake.* Several glasses of wine later, and the runaway train had gained speed to *Boys, get Dana to sing,* and eventually half the room had chanted until she set foot on the stage.

Things had just never really improved from the minute the word makeover had left Tara's lips until the second Dana stepped up to the mike and looked down on the face of her ex in amongst the crowd, disapproval written all over him.

Add to all that the fact that the make-believe game she was playing with Adam was proving entirely too easy and—dare she think it?—enjoyable, and really things couldn't get much more complicated.

He had smiled down at her with his impossibly attractive smile as she'd been pulled from his side by the people she had once called friends but probably never would again after this night. And as she had glanced back over her shoulder at him she had, for a very brief second, not wanted to leave him. 'Let's pretend' at its most convincing!

Billy, the lead guitarist with the band she'd regularly sung with at college, stepped forward to announce, 'This one'll bring back some memories for you lot. Guys, girls—give it up for Dana Lewis!'

She blinked for a moment at the use of her maiden

name, then the first soulful notes of an old blues song sounded up. Oh, great. A song with *innuendo*.

Of course. What else would it be in the nightmare from hell she was currently having? Okay, so it was one she'd sung on many different occasions, but not to a crowd that held an ex-husband who might read a lot into the lyrics and a 'date' who appeared to be convinced she was in love with the ex. A 'date' who was forcing her blood to thrum in her veins in ways she'd never before experienced.

She took a deep breath, closed her eyes to shut out the surreal place she was currently visiting, and began to sing.

Adam shut his mouth when it occurred to him he must look like a child who'd just been told Santa didn't exist. Who the hell was this multiple-personalitied woman?

The Dana he worked with every day sure as hell didn't look like the kind of woman who would stand on a stage and sing like that. Her voice was husky, sultry. In fact, in the dictionary under 'sexy' it probably said 'listen to Dana Taylor sing'. The sound went straight from his ears to—well, much further south than his ears, and he was stunned by his own reaction.

She slipped a hand up to caress the mikestand, up and down, and his mouth went dry. Dear God.

Her hips swayed slightly as she tilted her head and stepped one foot out to the side. The long slit in the side of her dress allowed a long, glorious, illegal-in-most-countries length of leg to be exposed to the room. Adam gulped and glanced around at the number of men looking up at her. He felt a sudden need to run up and cover her with something—*anything* that would shield her from their prying gazes.

She opened her eyes and looked directly at him,

damped her lips with the end of her now familiar pink tongue and sang directly at him, her eyes burning him from across the room.

He stepped closer, drawn in by the small smile she gave him. Then her eyes moved and he followed her line of vision to the tall fair-haired man near the back of the crowd. So that would be *him*, then.

His eyes moved back to her. She threw her long, dark, curled hair back over one shoulder with a flick of her head, her eyes shining with—what? Anger? Pain? Adam wasn't sure he wanted to know which.

There was clear innuendo in the words of the song as she sang them—to *him*?—then turned her gaze back to the remainder of the crowd, closing her eyes and raising her arms slightly with a shrug of her naked shoulders as she continued.

Had she chosen to sing that song specifically for *him*? The ex? The one she claimed she wasn't still in love with? And why the hell did he, Adam, care all of a sudden if she was or wasn't?

His whole plan of keeping on reminding himself that this was Dana Taylor, who he knew and couldn't spend any great amount of time with, just wasn't working for him. Because it was now more than apparent that he didn't actually know her at all. Not beyond the outer shell she'd permitted him to see. And knowing that fact bugged the hell out of Adam. He didn't like being behind in the game.

He glanced across at the ex again, and then started to walk towards the side of the stage. A primal, possessive instinct was kicking in. Suddenly he needed to be between Dana and the man she'd once been married to.

Side-stepping smiling women and the odd nod from a few men, he let his eyes rove back over her.

She tilted her head back as she took another breath to sing, and some invisible being dimmed the lights and threw a spotlight on her. Damn that dress. How was a red-blooded male supposed to resist her in it?

It seemed to shimmer as she moved, and the deep folds of material surrounding the V which cut halfway down her ribcage from stringy straps moved as she did. The movement almost, but not quite, revealed the rounded shapes the material barely covered. The suggestion was proving heating enough...

She turned her head as she sang, searching out his eyes in the crowd again, one eyebrow raised slightly at his approach.

He grinned a wide grin and lifted his chin in challenge. *Go on, Dana, give it your best shot.*

Dana smiled, suddenly enjoying the moment. To hell with the innuendo of the words. People could read whatever they wanted into them. She was having fun. She was remembering what it was like to be Dana the woman again. And it had been a long time since anyone had looked at her as Adam Donovan was doing right that minute.

Unbidden she could hear the faint sound of her sisters' voices in her ears. They were there, in the background, as they had been for months now. Encouraging her to live for the moment. To *feel* like a woman. Her unconscious night-time dreams had done several things with those suggestions over the months, but she'd never expected to come so close to those fantasies in real life. And certainly not with someone she disliked so strongly.

She turned towards him as she sang, tilting her head slightly forward so that her hair fell, tousled around her face. With a small smile she looked up at him from beneath long darkened lashes. Oh, yes. She could play this game just as well as she now knew he could. Adam who? He was just some guy, right? She could damn well live for the moment if she put her mind to it.

Adam stopped at the foot of the steps, pushed his hands deep into his trouser pockets and watched her. She was good. Up on that stage she was someone else. Someone he'd have wanted from the moment he set eyes on her. The game was holding a hell of a lot more interest for him now.

He flicked his glance back towards the ex again. 'In your face' material, the anally retentive Dana had requested. He turned his glance back to hers and slowly smiled. He knew how to get that result for her. Oh, she'd get what she'd wanted. As the saying went, *Be careful what you wish for…*

She lifted the mike out of its stand and moved towards him as she sang the last few bars of the song. Then as the music ended she handed the mike to Billy, glided elegantly down the steps, her eyes locked with Adam's, and found herself immediately swept up into a kiss.

The applause eventually seemed to die down as he held her and continued moving his mouth across hers. She actually tasted as good as she looked. He tilted his chin and moved a hand up to cup the back of her head and hold her closer. The other hand moved to the skin of her back, circled, turned over, knuckles running along her spine. He felt her shiver.

The band began playing another melancholy number and he swayed their bodies to the rhythm.

He smiled as he raised his head and waited patiently for her eyes to open. Then, tilting his head close again, he watched as his breath moved the wisps of hair around her cheeks. 'Who are you?'

She moved her tongue again, as if tasting him on her

lips, then small white teeth bit slightly at her lower lip. 'You mean you don't know?'

'I thought I did.'

She blinked her blue eyes at him. 'Does anyone ever know anyone, really?'

Adam considered her words. 'Maybe not.'

Without thinking about it she reached up to brush his heavy fringe back from his forehead. Yes, indeed. That trick of his worked well. She could feel the strong pull of her feminine side to his masculinity. Was this what her siblings had meant? The tug was strong. Hard to fight against.

'This isn't me, and you and I both know it.'

'Yes.' He nodded and continued smiling at her, an almost boyish smile. 'But that's the game, isn't it? You don't know me; I don't know you. That's what tonight is.'

That was the agreement.

Suddenly Dana didn't give a damn about Jim, or the perfect Melanie, or anyone else in the room. Maybe it was the alcohol; maybe it was just being swept along by the moment. Whatever it was, it was potent. It was irresistible.

She looked up at Adam's face. His gorgeous, appealing face. She'd never denied he was an attractive man. Back in the real world, she might not like his personality much, but his looks couldn't be denied. Not by any female with a pulse.

As his hand continued its movement along her naked skin her eyes grew heavy. She'd forgotten how seductive seduction could be. Not that she'd ever experienced it on this scale. Could she do it? Forget for one night that she was a sensible, rational-thinking person and just be a woman? A *femme fatale*? How many chances would she get in her lifetime?

With a sudden burst of clarity she realised it actually made sense. It wasn't as if she could deny the way her body was reacting to Adam. She—reluctantly—also couldn't deny the fact that he was a very attractive male. A very attractive, confirmed bachelor male. Perfect for the momentary fling her sisters had suggested and she had fantasised about. She didn't want another involvement anyway. So someone as obviously relationship-phobic as Adam was perfect, wasn't he? And better the devil she knew, right? There wasn't anything more complicated in it than that.

She'd consumed enough wine to give her courage, but not enough to use as an excuse. She stepped in closer and pressed herself against his chest as she whispered into his ear. 'So, how far does this little game go in that sordid mind of yours?'

He smiled a slow, sexy, dimpled smile. 'You really want to know?'

Not in the cold light of day she wouldn't. But she was currently in the realms of fantasyland. The thing was, could she live with the inevitable consequences of this one night when the sun came up again? Guilt, recrimination, regret? Working in an office with the person she'd 'flung' with?

She thought about how good it had felt to stand on that stage again, to watch the reactions on people's faces. On Adam's face. Was it so bad to want to feel like a woman again? To *not* be Dana the ex-wife, Dana the single parent, Dana the highly organised office manager, Dana the anally retentive...

Didn't every woman want to have one night where she could get lost in the feeling of being a woman? And those moments should just be taken where they could be found. Regardless of who the person was and how wrong they were in every other way. The moment might never happen again, might it?

Dana didn't need to get hurt again. To be a failure in a relationship again. And with Adam there was no question of there being a relationship, or anything even slightly more long-lasting than ice cream left out of the freezer compartment. It was ideal.

'You're the master at this stuff, Adam. This is your usual turf, unless I'm mistaken.' She brought her head close until her nose almost touched the end of his. 'Well, we *could* play it like this: you promise to forget everything about tonight, you never mention it again even if we're alone, and after the fact we'll simply go back to that comfortable antagonism we have for each other.'

He raised an eyebrow as he followed her train of thought. 'Where it's safe?'

She nodded. 'Yes.'

'And if I agree?'

The Dana of old peeked out of her cage and smiled. She moved her head in, lightly kissing him, and whispered, 'Then we'll just play this game for the rest of the night and see where it leads us.'

The atmosphere in the office sucked.

There was just no other way of putting it. They'd managed to be unbearably polite to each other for the first week, but by the second week had progressed to a small amount of sniping at each other. Week three had turned to out-and-out sarcasm, and by week four they could barely manage a civil conversation.

By halfway through week five Dana was exhausted by the whole thing. Tired to the bone, in fact, and she had the beginnings of an absolute darling of a stomach flu if her reaction to anything fried was anything to go by.

Adam was tucking into a bacon sandwich when he noticed how pale she'd gone. He studied her as he chewed. It was something he seemed to spend more and more time doing these days. Studying Dana, that was. Not chewing.

It was just that sometimes he had to really think in order to conjure up a mental image of the other Dana on the reunion night. That amazing, intriguing, sexy woman he'd spent the make-believe night with. Where in hell had she gone? Because by the time he'd walked back into the office on Monday Little Miss Perfect was back and in 'spring clean' mode. He hated that side of her all the more now that he knew what she could be.

So he found himself looking for the other her. He looked every day. And he'd yet to see so much as a glimpse of her. In a weird way he missed her.

Dana glanced up from her paperwork and frowned at him. 'Do you have to eat that thing in here?'

'Yep.' He answered with his mouth full, mostly because he knew how much that irritated her.

'Most people eat *before* they come to work. It's called breakfast, and traditionally it's eaten at home so that bits of it don't end up all over planning applications.'

He grinned and took another large bite. 'I'm not most people.'

Her eyes watched as he licked the crumbs from his lips and her stomach flip-flopped. It had to be the flu, because she'd managed to ban images of anything else from her mind. Every time they threatened to revisit her she would think about shopping lists, or famous designers, or the number of people in her family and their dates of birth. She could stick to the arrangement. She damn well could.

After all, memories of that night didn't seem to enter Adam's head at all.

She shook her head and stood to retrieve a copy of the planning application guide for the area of their latest project. They'd had three enquiries since the reunion, so at least something good had come from the whole thing.

As she pulled the drawer open the room began to spin slightly.

*Oh, no.*

A resolutely chewing Adam watched her back as she swayed. He chewed and swallowed. 'You okay?'

'I'm fine.' She frowned over her shoulder, dragged out the required file and was turning to get back to her seat when she swayed again.

*Oh-oh.*

Adam was out of his seat like a bullet, and had caught her before she hit the ground. He noticed again how pale she'd gone as he swept her up into his arms to carry her to the large sofa on one side of the room.

Once she was lying down he propped pillows behind her head, hunched down beside her, and called her name softly until she opened her eyes. When she did he almost sighed with relief. 'Hey, there.'

She blinked at the intimate tone of his voice. She remembered that tone. She knew she wasn't supposed to remember, but she did. She blinked again. 'Hey.'

'How long have you been sick, oh invincible one?'

Her first instinct was to lie, but with his thumb rubbing across her knuckles and concern in his green eyes she found she couldn't. 'A week or so. It's no big deal. Just a virus of some kind.'

The ends of a frown appeared beneath the fringe that had fallen forward. 'That's why you've had a problem with my breakfast in the office?'

Dana took a shaky breath and blinked to hold back a completely uncalled-for wave of tears. She couldn't cope if he was going to be nice to her.

He shook his head. 'You should have said.'

Her eyebrow quirked slightly.

'Okay, I'd have been sarcastic about it—but I'd have stopped.' His dimples appeared at her look of disbelief. 'Well, I'd have stopped until you were better.'

Consideration wasn't proving a good thing either. Lord, she must really be tired if he was able to choke her up so easily. She was usually much stronger. She attempted to struggle upwards but found herself pinned down with one long arm. 'Let me up, Adam, I'm fine.'

'You've fainted before today?'

'No.'

The answer was too quick. 'How many times?'

She sighed. '*Hell.* Twice. I'm just run down. We've been busy, Jess has had a cold, and I'm tired. So I've caught something. It'll be fine.'

'Okay.' He stood and pointed down at her. 'Don't move.'

'Where are you going?' Her guarded eyes watched as he marched across to his desk and lifted the phone. 'Who are you calling?'

'What's your doctor's name?'

She moved to swing her legs off the edge of the sofa.

'Don't get up, Dana—I mean it!' The sharp tone to his voice sent her further back into the sofa's cushions. '*Name.*'

'I can get to the doctor's on my own.' She pouted over at him.

His eyes softened slightly at her huff. It was vaguely cute. 'Yeah, and that's why you've seen him already and got antibiotics or something for this?'

'My being sick is none of your damn business.'

'It is if it affects your work. And I'd say passing out in the office qualifies, wouldn't you?' He waved the receiver back and forward beside him. 'Name and number.'

Dana narrowed her eyes at him. She folded her arms across her breasts and sighed. 'Kennedy, and she's at the Health Centre.' She glared across at him. 'And I'm damn well going on my own.'

He flipped open a local directory and punched in the number.

With the receiver propped between his shoulder and his ear he smiled sweetly across at her. 'The hell you are.'

Dana blinked at her doctor. 'I can't be.'

'You can, apparently.'

'No, really. I can't be.'

The doctor was a patient woman. She set her pen on her desk and smiled. 'Well, you are. Just over five weeks, I'd say.'

Dana laughed nervously. Oh, she knew the date. 'No, you see, I *can't* be because we used precautions.' A miracle in itself at the time, considering how fast everything had happened, but still. 'We were *safe*.'

'Well, nothing is a hundred per cent safe.'

'Then it should say that on the box!' She jumped back slightly at the sharpness of her own voice. 'I'm sorry.' She adjusted her tone. 'But it bloody well should do.'

The older woman continued to smile patiently. 'It does.'

Dana shook her head. 'Then it should say it in clearer print or bigger letters—or at least larger than the manufacturer's name!'

'I take it this is unplanned, then?'

That was certainly one way of putting it. This whole

consequences thing was way bigger than she could ever have foreseen at the time. After all, a baby? A baby with Adam Donovan? Oh, dear God.

She moaned and placed her head in her hands. 'This just isn't happening to me.' She peeked out from behind her fingers. 'You're really, really sure? I mean absolutely positive, no pun intended?'

A nod. 'Well, obviously we have to send your sample away to confirm it, but these tests are pretty foolproof now, and I have seen a few of these cases before.'

'Of course you have.'

The woman's eyes examined her carefully until she reappeared from behind her hands. 'What about the father? Will he be involved?'

Dana wanted to throw up. She really, truly did. *The father* was currently sitting in the waiting room, waiting for her to come out. He hadn't trusted her enough to walk into an elevator and into the surgery. She actually laughed aloud. Oh, boy, was he in for a surprise.

If she told him.

'I think I need to think about this for a while.'

'Of course you do.' Dr Kennedy turned towards her desk and wrote out a prescription. 'I'm giving you the usual folic acid, and a course of iron and some vitamins. You're a little underweight at the minute, so you know you need to rest and be cautious. I'll expect to see you in a couple of weeks' time to arrange antenatal care and a scan.'

Dana nodded. 'I know.' She took the prescription and opened her mouth. Then closed it. What was she going to say after all? Thank you? Oh, yes. *Thank you for the most devastating news of my life. Thanks a bunch.*

But it wasn't the doctor's fault, after all. *She* hadn't

advised her to do the whole 'live out your fantasy and be a woman for just one night' thing.

'I'll call.'

'Good. Look after yourself, Dana. You know the score, here.'

She pulled the door closed behind her and stood in the corridor for long, long moments. At the end of the corridor was the waiting room. In the waiting room was Adam. Adam Donovan. Officially the most annoying man on the planet. The world's most confirmed bachelor.

The father of her baby.

She reached a hand down and held it over her flat abdomen. She'd always been a believer in the idea that everything happened for a reason. But somebody sure did believe in testing her faith. She was also now going to have to kill every single one of her sisters for planting such a damn stupid idea in her fertile imagination to begin with.

She took a deep breath and walked down the corridor.

# CHAPTER FOUR

ADAM kept watching the doorway. He'd been watching it for fifteen minutes solid, since Dana had disappeared through it. After about two minutes he'd started to worry a little. After five he'd admitted to himself he was worried. At seven he had looked deeper and realised that admitting he was worried meant in some small way that he must care. That thought alone had made him stop thinking completely for the eighth minute.

By ten he'd been pacing. Fine. He did care. He hated the fact that he cared, but he did. Even someone as irritating as Dana was capable of burrowing their way under a person's skin, he realised. It was just that he'd got kind of used to her being around. There was a familiarity in her irritating ways.

Maybe if they both made an effort they could be, like, friends or something. After all, he'd been best pals with Jack for years now. He could have Jack's sister as a friend, he guessed. Well, he could give it a try. If he worked at it really hard and she did the same...

But what if somewhere during their friendship *she* reappeared? That other Dana—the fantasy Dana. What then? He stopped pacing. That wouldn't be a good thing. Well, maybe *good* was the wrong word to use there.

It just wouldn't be *safe*. Yeah, that was a better description.

After all, Adam was Mister Free and Single. Last bastion of the bachelor race. He'd set himself a goal of staying single indefinitely. And if the fantasy Dana came back he'd be in big, big trouble.

She walked out through the door, glared at him, and marched towards the elevator.

Adam caught up with her in about three strides. 'Well? What did she say?'

'I'll live.'

He watched her punch the elevator button with enough force to dislocate her thumb. 'And it's the flu?'

She laughed, the sound a tad hysterical to her own ears. 'Oh, yeah, the flu. Yep, that's exactly what it is.'

The elevator doors slid open and she marched inside, turned and leaned back against the wall. She avoided looking at him as he followed her in, instead folding her arms across her chest and staring straight ahead.

Adam pushed the button marked 'G' and then leaned on the side wall. He glanced at the paper half folded and gripped tightly in her hand. 'She gave you a prescription? I'll get that for you.'

She looked at him with wide eyes. 'Oh, no, you won't.'

'It's only a prescription, Dana. I'll get it on the way back and then you can get started on it straight away.'

She unfolded her arms and glared down at the piece of paper, then back up at him. 'No. *I'll* get it.'

He watched as she frantically patted her trousers and shirt in search of a pocket to hide the offending item in. He stepped towards her. 'You'll say you're too busy to get it and then you'll end up sick for weeks.'

Oh, if only he knew. 'Would you stop trying to be nice to me? I don't like it.'

He frowned at her as she transferred the paper to the hand furthest from him. Side-stepping, he reached for it again.

'I'm not trying to be nice. I'm trying to be sensible.

You and I both know you're crap at looking after yourself when you get sick. Last time you had a cold it lasted a month because you wouldn't take the time to swallow a vitamin C tablet.'

'It had to work its course, that was all.' Sort of as this would have to. She transferred the paper back to the other hand and then hid the hand behind her back. 'I'll get this later.'

'We'll get it on the way back to the office.' He frowned, darted right, and when she leaned away reached with his other hand and snatched the paper from the hand behind her back. He smiled in victory. 'The sooner you start taking this stuff—' he waved the paper in front of her face '—the sooner you'll get better.'

Dana stared in horror as, turning slightly towards the doors, he glanced down at the prescription in his hands. She pushed herself further back against the metal wall, hoping it would open up and suck her in.

The doors slid open at their floor as the frown appeared on his forehead. He didn't move. Just put out a hand to stop her, and glanced up at her as the doors slid closed again.

'Folic acid?'

She swallowed hard.

Adam continued to frown, looked down at the writing as if he'd read it wrong, and then looked into her pale face again. 'Folic acid, and iron and vitamin supplements?'

Dana nodded.

'For the flu?'

Her heart was beating so hard she felt convinced it was echoing around what currently felt like the tiniest elevator in the world.

He stared at her. 'It's not for the flu, is it?'

Dana ever so slowly shook her head.

His eyes dropped down to her stomach and then back up. 'We were careful.'

She managed to find a small, squeaking voice. 'Not careful enough, apparently.'

'But we used—'

'I *know*. I was *there*.' She frowned at him. 'But apparently those things aren't a hundred per cent reliable. So my doctor informs me.'

Adam scowled. 'That should be written somewhere, then, don't you think?' Not that he'd ever read the package before.

She actually smiled a small smile. 'That's somewhat similar to what I said.'

They stared at each other as the elevator opened its doors on the surgery level. Without glancing round, Adam stretched back and pushed the button again. He searched her face, noting the defeat in her eyes and the shadows that betrayed her tiredness. She was pregnant. *They* were pregnant.

'Were you going to tell me?'

She shrugged, but continued to look up at him. 'I don't honestly know. I needed some time to think, I guess.'

He nodded, looked down at his feet, then looked back up again. 'Are you going to have it?'

Did he mean was she going to get rid of if? Oh, that would just let him right off the hook wouldn't it? He could continue right on with his bachelor lifestyle and never look back.

The mother instinct in her kicked in. Well, she jolly well wouldn't need to get rid of *her* baby for that to happen. The doors swooshed open and she glared at him with flashing eyes.

'Oh, don't worry, Adam. I won't be expecting you to

be present at the birth or its first day at university or anything in the in-between. You can just pretend it never happened and go on living that free and easy life of yours.'

He frowned down at her as she pushed out past him and marched through the foyer. Damn the woman. He'd never met anyone who could jump to the wrong conclusion as fast as she could.

As she hit the open air his hand captured her elbow, halting her escape. He swung her to face him. 'You really hate my guts, don't you?'

She tried to wrestle her arm free. 'Right now I'm not exactly your number one fan, no!'

He tightened his hold. 'No, I don't mean right now. I mean ever since you first met me. You hadn't even known me five seconds and you already looked at me like I was pond scum. What exactly is your problem with me?'

'Some people just don't click with other people.'

He ignored her attempts to pull free, steering her across the street to the car park and his car. 'No, that's not it. There's something more behind it. And you know what, Dana?' He stopped to glare down at her. 'It may have been amusing for a time, but this last while it's been getting pretty damned tired. So why don't you just tell me what the problem is?'

'Problem? You mean *apart* from the pregnancy?'

He shook his head. 'You're keeping this baby?'

She blinked back another threatened onslaught of tears and nodded. There was no way he could possibly understand her feelings on this. Not without knowing more of her past. And look where opening up had got her last time. 'Like I said, that's not your problem. Fatherhood is hardly at the top of your priority list.'

He ignored the jibe. 'If you're keeping this baby then

you don't hate me as much as you'd like to think you do. Because this baby is half *me*. And if you honestly think for one second I could spend my life wandering around knowing I have a child and having nothing to do with its life, then you really haven't the faintest idea of the kind of person I am.'

Dana stood statue-still as his words washed over her. She didn't even realise he'd released her until he turned and walked away to unlock his car.

After a few long moments he raised his eyes and looked across at her, leaning his arms across the roof of the car. 'You getting in?'

She blinked as thoughts moved round and round in her poor crowded head. For a blind second she even wondered whether, if she were to try pinching herself, she would wake up.

Slowly her feet began to move her towards the car. 'How exactly do you see this working, Adam?'

He shrugged. 'Like I have any clue? I've no experience in the parenting department, Dana. But I won't let you do this alone. So you may as well just get used to that.'

Her feet stopped when she was able to place her arms on the roof, the same as his. 'You don't have to.'

The green of his eyes softened slightly. 'I think I do.'

'You already know you're not my favourite person on the planet.'

Adam took a breath. 'You hate my guts.'

She shook her head. 'No, you're right in what you said. I don't hate you completely. If I hated you that much you'd never have got close enough to make this baby.'

His heart beat slightly out of rhythm. It was quite a confession from her. And also the first time they'd made any reference to the night they'd sworn never to talk about. 'You were different that night.'

'Yes, I was.'

'The thing is, Dana, whatever your reasons for being different that night, the fact is *I* wasn't. I was still me and it was me you made love with.'

Dana felt her chest tighten at his soft words. He was right. There had been nothing different about Adam that night apart from the fact that she'd set all the things that bugged her most about him to one side. She'd let go of her prejudices and for one night lived out a fantasy or two.

'There's no future for you and me.'

He stared at her, took a breath, then brushed his fringe back with long fingers. 'We made a baby. There's a future with you and me in it whether you like it or not.'

'Are you looking forward to being a dad?'

Jack grinned across at Adam as they lifted the newly assembled cot into place in the newly finished nursery. 'You can't tell? It's better than Christmas.'

Adam couldn't resist teasing him. 'You're only pleased because you'll have someone the same mental age as you in the house.'

'Well, you're here now, so at least I'm not lonely.'

They pushed the furniture into place and stood back to survey the room. Jack smiled ridiculously while Adam looked from fluffy bunny to wooden alphabet letters.

A small wave of panic crossed his chest.

This stuff was happening to him too. That was why it had seemed the right idea to pick Jack's brain on the subject. Not that he could make it too obvious.

After all, Jack was his best friend. And Adam wanted to keep it that way. But somehow he figured if he were to mention he'd got one of Jack's sisters pregnant on a one-night stand their relationship might change slightly. Once he got out of hospital, anyway.

'Tara okay?'

Jack glanced at his friend's profile. 'Okay with being pregnant or okay healthwise?'

Adam shrugged and continued looking around the room with a conscious expression of uninterest. 'Both, I guess.'

'Why?'

He glanced sideways at his friend's small smile. 'Can't I just ask out of curiosity? I happen to like your wife.'

'Mmm.' Jack nodded. 'Just so long as it's from a distance.'

'I wouldn't even think it.'

'Well, I can see how the pregnancy thing might be a bit of a turn-off for you. Pregnant women aren't really your type, are they?'

Adam had to concentrate really hard on a large red letter 'C' for a moment, to keep his face straight. 'Not normally, no.'

'Don't tell me you're changing your type. What's wrong? You worn out all the other avenues?'

'That's funny, Jack.'

'Yeah.' Jack slapped him on the back in a guy kind of way. 'I'm a funny man. That wife of mine tells me so all the time.'

'Are you sure she means funny *amusing*?'

'I like to hope it's what she means.'

Side by side they turned and left the bright room to amble along the hallway. Adam looked around him at the home his friend had created for his new family. The place had been a wreck when he'd bought it, but now it was warm, comfortable. The minute a person walked in they felt cocooned in a safe haven. Adam guessed that was how a home was supposed to feel. It was certainly how his had felt growing up. Which really didn't explain why he hadn't felt the need to go out and build a similar life for himself. Maybe he was just weird.

'So why the sudden interest?'

Adam glanced ahead as Jack's words sounded in his left ear. He shrugged again. 'Curious, I guess. Not like I know much on the subject.' He smiled sideways. 'And I may need to know some stuff for when Tara leaves you to run away with me.'

Jack smiled slightly at the teasing. 'I'd hunt you both down and drag her right back. Ain't no kid of mine being raised by a playboy like you. Those two are my life now, and nothing would keep me from them.'

They stopped at the top of the stairs and Adam mulled over Jack's words before asking, 'You think I'd make a crap father?'

Jack looked stunned. 'You *care*? Since when have you even thought about being a father? Not that I haven't wondered how you've managed to escape it for so long, what with the law of averages and all that.'

Adam frowned at his friend. 'You make it sound like I've slept with half the country.'

Jack's eyebrow raised in an all too familiar manner. A Lewis family trait, obviously. 'You haven't?'

Well, hell, he'd been around *some*, yeah. But it wasn't as if the figure had hit huge numbers. Some of them hadn't even lasted beyond a first date. 'I didn't sleep with every woman I dated, Jack, and in case you'd forgotten we were building a business for a long time there.'

'Yes, I remember. But it's not like you've been lonely, is it?'

No. He'd had company when he wanted it. That had never been a problem. But he wasn't actually as loose-living as he supposed he'd painted himself. In fact he hadn't been loose the least little bit for quite some time. Practically monk-like, in actuality. The whole business had almost lost interest for him.

He frowned hard at the realisation.

Jack seemed to regret his words. 'It's not that I think you'd make a crap father, Adam, it's just that I've never remotely associated you with the *idea* of being a father. You having a mid-life crisis or some dumb thing?'

In his early thirties? 'No, but I may pencil one in, in a year or two, just to get it over and done with.'

'I guess we all think about it at some time. Fatherhood, I mean. It's built in.'

Adam raised an eyebrow and pushed his hands into the pockets of his worn jeans. 'Is that why you're having a baby?'

Jack smiled, a small flush touching his neck. 'Nope.'

'Okay, so why, then?'

'Honest answer or guy answer?'

'Honest one.'

The flush moved up to tinge Jack's cheeks and he shrugged a little self-consciously. 'I love my wife, Adam. I know you think I've let the side down, but I do. I love her, and I can't think of any better way to shout that to the world than to have a small version of her running around the place. One that's half me, half her.'

Adam blinked at him.

Jack grinned. 'Oh, yeah, go on—laugh it up, make with the one-liners. You do your worst, pal. I can take it. But it's how I feel and that's that. Long after I'm not here any more, my child will be walking around making mistakes of his or her own, laughing and loving through life. And I guess that kind of makes Tara and me into for ever.'

His words made sense. It wasn't that Adam had disagreed with the idea before. It was just that he'd never had to spend any actual time *thinking* about it before.

He returned to his original question. 'And Tara's okay?'

Jack was stunned by the simple, serious question. Something was up. He searched his friend's face but Adam was giving nothing away. Okay. He was a patient guy. He'd wait. It'd come out eventually. He smiled, though, as he answered. There was a woman involved somewhere…

'She gets tired, but she's stopped throwing up every day so that's good. But, being Tara, she needs to be sat on regularly to make sure she rests and eats right.' His chest puffed slightly. 'That's my job. Healthy mother means healthy baby. I'm also pretty damn good at the happy mother means happy baby thing too.'

Adam stepped down onto the top stair and continued his train of thought. 'So as long as she rests and looks after herself then they'll be okay? That's pretty much how it works?'

Jack followed him down. 'Well, yeah. I guess you worry a bit for the first few months, in case of miscarriages and all, but they can happen any time.'

Adam stopped and looked over his shoulder. 'There's no danger of that with Tara, though?' He knew they'd both be devastated to lose their baby. He had to search to see how he'd feel about the same thing.

Jack shook his head and walked round his friend. 'Nah, she's healthy as a horse. I think I was more nervous for her than she was, after everything that Dana went through all those years.'

Adam's stomach flipped. 'What?'

'Oh, yeah.' Jack clicked his fingers and stopped several stairs down to look back up at Adam's shocked face. 'I keep forgetting you two can't hold a civil conversation. You don't know, do you?'

'No, I guess I don't.' He swallowed and walked slowly downwards. 'So why don't you tell me, so I don't have to humiliate myself by asking?'

Jack seemed to consider it for several long moments. They were a close family. Private information wasn't always volunteered to others. But this was Adam; he was part of Jack's family in a way. Maybe knowing a little more about Dana's past would help him to improve their working relationship. Understanding could be a good thing…

'Dana tried for another baby when she was married to Jim. She really didn't want Jess to be an only child; it was important to her.'

That made sense. Adam had hated being an only child. It was the only actual complaint he had about his early years. He focused hard on the new information.

Jack took a deep breath. 'But some things just aren't meant to happen, I guess. And considering how bad things got when he ditched her I suppose it turned out for the best. But Dana didn't see it that way at the time. It broke her heart.'

Adam's eyes grew wide as the meaning behind the words sunk in. He felt a shiver down his back. *No.*

'She miscarried?'

Jack nodded. 'Twice.'

# CHAPTER FIVE

WHEN the front door opened he had to look down to make eye contact. A miniature Dana Taylor looked up at him with guarded eyes. The girl cocked her head to one side and raised an eyebrow at him. Definitely a Lewis trait, then.

'Hi.'

She stared up at him. That trait she obviously got from her mother too. Dana had been protective as all hell when it came to her daughter spending time in her working environment. Never the twain shall meet, kind of thing.

Adam grinned. 'You're Jess.'

'And you're Adam Donovan.'

'Yes, I am.'

'I've seen you before. You work with my mum.'

Adam's smile grew. 'Yes, I do.' She'd mentioned him, then.

'Mmm.' Jess smiled to herself. 'I've heard her say that some days she wishes you would crawl back under your rock.'

His smile faded. 'Where *is* your mother?'

'Out back.'

'Australia?'

Jess giggled. 'No, on the porch roof—out the back.'

On the roof? Dana was on a damned *roof*? With the baby?

Adam shook his head at his own thoughts as he jogged around the house. How on earth was she going to go anywhere *without* it?

70

As he rounded the edge of the stone farmhouse he located her walking a wobbly line along the edge of a flat roof that joined an old extension to the back of the building. She was wearing ripped blue overalls about three sizes too large and a baseball cap, with a ponytail that poked out back. She didn't look like her usual Little Miss Perfect. But that observation grew dim behind the important fact in Adam's mind that she was indeed *on a bloody roof*!

'What the hell do you think you're doing?'

She jumped at the sound of his voice and wobbled precariously as she turned to face him with wide eyes. 'What are *you* doing here?'

'Get down off that roof right now.' He strode towards her with an angry glare. 'How stupid are you?'

It was kind of an open-ended question, considering her current condition, but she managed to not point that out. Instead she set her bucket at her feet and pushed the peak of her hat back to frown properly at him. 'I will not get down off this roof. It's my roof. I'm *fixing* my roof. It's none of your business if I stand on twenty roofs a day.'

'It damn well is my business when you're—' His eyes caught sight of Jess through the window downstairs. He thought for a moment, then looked upwards. *'Not well.'*

She noticed the movement of his eyes. Her own eyes widened and she mouthed down at him, *'Jess?'*

He smiled over his gritted teeth and nodded. 'Get down off there. *Please.*'

'I can't.'

He raised an eyebrow. 'You're stuck?'

'No. I have to fix this roof. It's leaking.'

Adam took a deep breath and stepped forward. 'Then I'll fix it. You shouldn't be up on a roof.'

Dana planted a hand on one hip. 'What have you been doing? Studying up?'

He smiled dangerously. 'Get off the roof, Dana, or I'm going to come up there and get you off the roof.'

She stared down at him. He was serious. She could tell from the stubborn set of his wide shoulders and the dangerous glint in his eyes. Her female hormones were obviously kicking in with the new baby, because damn it if he didn't look sexy as hell down there.

He brushed his hand up and back to smooth his fringe into place, his eyes never leaving her. 'Well?'

Dana continued to study him. It *had* to be her hormones playing up. From her advantageous height looking down on him she was suddenly struck by how boyish he could look, with that thick, disobedient fringe of his and the dimples that appeared when he grinned. He had the ability to look about eighteen in a certain light.

She was suddenly hit by a mental vision of an even younger version of him, and her arm snaked around her stomach. Hormones could be devious sometimes.

'Do you even know *how* to fix a roof?'

'You won't know 'til you get down, will you?' He folded his arms across his chest and tilted his head, which dislodged his fringe again. 'And it's yet another of the many unanswered questions you must have, because you don't know me any better than I know you. Now, get your ass off the roof.'

She started to walk towards the edge of the porch, where a ladder was propped. 'I'm only getting down because I'm interested to see what you'll do with the roof.' Her eyes flicked down. 'Not because you're making me do it.'

'Fine.' He watched her every motion, shadowing her movements from the ground. 'Whatever works for you.'

Holding the steps firmly, he watched until her feet hit safe ground. He then placed two hands on her shoulders and turned her to face him. With one long finger he nudged the peak of her hat up so he could see her properly. 'Promise you won't do anything all *independent woman* this next while.'

Her lips pursed slightly and she frowned. 'I do the jobs that I can do myself because it's cheaper that way. I'm not out to prove anything.'

Adam smiled. 'Sure you're not. But you have to look out for yourself now.' He looked down at her overall-covered stomach before looking back into her eyes, his voice low. 'For both of you.'

Dana's mouth went dry. Oh, good Lord above, those hormones were busy. She blinked up at him. 'I'm fine. You don't have to pull the protective routine, Adam, really.'

He smiled. 'Tough.'

He glanced up at the roof and around at the house in general. 'I want a list of all the things that need to be done at any height.' He glanced back at her with a look of suspicion. 'Inside *and* out.' He thought some more. 'And of any heavy lifting jobs.'

'Can I go to the bathroom on my own?'

He smiled. 'Yes, that you can most definitely do.'

Technically unable to move while his bulk was in her way, she asked him the next obvious question. 'Are you planning on doing this for the next seven-odd months?'

'I guess I am.'

'Won't that cramp your love-life just a tad?'

And she thought becoming a father wouldn't? 'I guess that's my choice, isn't it?'

She continued to blink up at him. The thought of him being there, attempting to take care of her in his own particular way for the next seven months, was much scarier than being pregnant. It was amazing what guilt could do to a grown man's conscience. Well, if he wanted to take care of all those little chores for her and play househelp for a while, then that was fine. She'd make sure he got sick of it real fast.

With a small smile she fluttered her eyelashes. 'Okay, then, I'll make you a list, Adam. Your wish is my command.'

He stepped back to allow her to squeeze past him. He'd won. Kind of. So why did it feel as if he'd just been outwitted? If she was doing that damned devious thing of hers on him he'd strangle her.

Dana began to feel vaguely guilty as the light started to dim outside. He'd been working for hours. In fact he was fairly dedicatedly working his way through the list.

And Dana had put things on that list she would never ever have attempted on her own...

The last time she'd looked out at him he'd been trying to unstick bits of sawdust—created when he'd sawn wood to replace the loose panelling on the bottom half of her back door—from the bitumen that had dried like glue to his shirt when he'd done the porch roof. He'd been frowning in concentration, and had sworn quite loudly a couple of times when he'd dropped something or hit himself with a hammer, but in general Dana was quietly impressed by his businesslike attitude to it all.

The thought had occurred to her that he could, when he really tried, be a vaguely nice guy. She shook her head as she sat down to pay some bills in her living room. The *All Things Good* list was getting slightly longer. She was really going to have to consider goading him into another argument in order to dislike him again.

With a sigh she wrote a cheque and pushed her paper-work back so she could swing her legs onto the sofa. She'd forgotten how tiring it could be in the early stages of being pregnant. Well, that and the whole stress of ac-tually *being* pregnant and how it had happened. Not a good combination at all—at least not for her.

Her hand strayed to her flat stomach and she sent a silent plea upwards. She wanted this one. It would never make up for the ones she'd lost, but she really wanted this one.

Given the choice, she wouldn't have gone out and asked for it. Not with him. But it was here now. A part of her. A part of a night she hadn't been able to forget, no matter how hard she'd tried. If she'd known the con-sequences of giving in to lust for one night would be so big, would she still have given in?

Her eyes grew heavy. If it hadn't been with Adam things would certainly have been less complicated. But maybe this was her last chance. Maybe she would never get another opportunity to repeat the joy she had being Jess's mother. Her hand moved in a soothing circle.

She wanted this baby. And, she thought with a small smile as she drifted into sleep, it wouldn't be so very bad if it was as good-looking as its father.

It was Jess who directed him towards the living room when it got dark. She'd been a sort of builder's mate for most of the afternoon, pointing out where things were amid the chaos that was their workshed.

Adam had found her easier to talk to than her mother—less complicated than he had supposed. He could chat to a kid. That had reassured him a bit. If the baby was born as a ten-year-old he would be fine.

The interior of the house was chaotic, and Adam found

himself grinning as he walked through to the front room. For someone who was so completely anally retentive at work, Dana lived a lifestyle at the opposite end of the scale at home.

Each room was stuffed with worn, comfortable furniture in varying bright colours, many pieces of which by law should clash but somehow didn't. There were books, toys, and piles of laundry here and there. On the walls there were old kids' drawings, photos, and the odd painting that somehow Adam just knew was Dana's own work. He grinned a little more. He quite liked her house. It was more like the other Dana. The one he'd made a baby with.

When he ducked down to walk through a low-beamed doorway he found her curled up on the sofa, sleeping. The grin disappeared and he leaned back on his heels to watch her.

She was beautiful. Really, absolutely stunning. He'd heard that most pregnant women were, but also accepted that he possibly hadn't allowed himself to really look at her much. Well, that night set aside. But then that was 'other Dana' territory again.

Work Dana was all neat and precise and polished. This Dana was all ruffled and soft and sexy.

He walked silently across the room and hunkered down beside her. His eyes moved over her dark hair, where it had escaped from the ponytail in wispy tendrils around her face. Reaching out, he turned a tendril between his fingers, twisting it into a curl like she'd worn the night of the reunion. He let his eyes wander over the smooth skin of her forehead, the gentle arch of her eyebrows, and down over the long lashes that lay against her slightly flushed cheeks.

Then he looked at her mouth, her pink-lipped, slightly open mouth. And he remembered.

His body remembered too. He let go of her hair and stood up to walk a few steps away. This had to be the trap he'd always heard so much about. That thing where a single guy started to get sucked in by a woman.

Adam had managed to avoid it up until now, but, man, was the tug of it strong. He moved out of the room.

The front door knocker sounded as he pulled the living room door quietly closed.

Without thinking he turned and opened the heavier door. Jim Taylor looked him straight in the eye.

Adam looked straight back at him. 'Can I help you?'

'You're Adam?'

Adam nodded. Yeah, he'd have wanted to know who he was after the reunion night too, if he'd been the ex.

Jim reached out a hand. 'I'm—'

Adam ignored the offered hand. 'I know who you are.'

He felt himself rise slightly, to fill the small doorway a little more. It was the most ridiculous of primal urges— but, hey, he was *in* the house, Jim was *out* of it. Adam discovered he quite liked it that way. And anyway, he reasoned inwardly, he had a right to be here now.

Jim pulled back his hand and stood slightly taller himself. As they were of similar height and build, it became a very visible stand-off. The slightly fairer-haired man raised his chin. 'Is Dana home?'

'She's sleeping.' Adam smiled in a way he hoped would be interpreted as 'because I tired her out'. 'She must have forgotten you were calling over.'

'She didn't forget.' Jim's eyes remained cool in their study of Adam's face. 'Jess left some school things at our place yesterday, so I've brought them by.'

Of course he had. Adam wondered if he brought things by on a regular basis. He discovered he didn't like that idea.

The door to his right opened and a sleepy-eyed Dana appeared at his side. She glanced at Adam with a small frown. 'How long was I asleep?'

With a soft smile he turned his head and looked down at her. 'Not that long, babes.'

*Babes?* She raised an eyebrow at him, opening her mouth for a suitable retort. But a movement caught her eye past his shoulder and she looked over at the other man. 'Jim!'

Jim smiled at her wide eyes. 'Hi.'

Dana blinked at him, then looked at Adam, then back at Jim.

Oh, this was interesting. She cleared her throat. 'You've met Adam, then?'

'Yes, I have.'

'We were just getting acquainted.'

That was nice. Dana blinked at Jim with suspicion. 'What are you doing here?'

Ah. So he *didn't* just bring things by on a regular basis. Adam smiled at her. *Good girl.*

'Jess left some school stuff behind.' He held up a bag in his defence. 'So I thought I'd bring it by.'

Dana unconsciously reached up a hand to smooth her hair back into place. Her eyes flickered up to meet Adam's and she frowned slightly as he smiled at her. Then, out of nowhere, he reached over and pulled her into the crook of his arm. 'That was thoughtful of Jim—wasn't it, babes?'

Unusually so, if truth be known. It would never have occurred to him to deliver it before. With his busy schedule? No, that was why Dana seemed to spend half her life driving into town to collect Jess's belongings.

Jim's eyes moved backwards and forwards from Adam

to Dana. 'Not a problem. In fact, I'll be popping in more often, I hope.'

Dana gaped at him. He would?

Adam frowned at him. Would he hell!

Dana managed to force out the words. 'Why would you do that, exactly?'

'Because I'd like to see more of Jess.'

He hadn't wanted to see more of Jess in the four years since they'd finally agreed on visitation rights. Her eyes narrowed. 'Why?'

Adam actually understood why. For some inexplicable reason it was clear as day to him. If *his* child was getting a prospective new father figure in her life, he'd damn well want to check them out too.

He blinked as his mind continued to put little jigsaw pieces together. Now he was looking at himself as an additional father for Jess? Well, hell, why not roll in a few dozen cousins for him to be paternal to as well? After all, his life had been just tripping over with children to date, so it wasn't like a few dozen more would make a difference.

But at the same time Adam also knew he didn't like the idea of good old Jim being involved in his baby's life. Or, it would seem, Dana's life for that matter. Now, what the hell was with *that*? He was going all protective. That trap was closing in on him, it really was.

'I think recently I've realised how much I've been missing.'

Adam squeezed Dana a little tighter to his side. Jim had better not mean what Adam thought he meant with that line.

'I'm sure Jess will like that,' he said.

Dana looked at him in surprise. 'You think it would be a good idea to have Jim visit more?'

Well, if he was completely honest...

'For Jess. Fathers should spend time with their kids. You *know* I think that.' His eyes transferred his exact meaning to her.

Dana knew he wasn't just referring to Jess. 'Yes, I know you think that. And if the father has shown that kind of enthusiasm from the start, then that's a good thing.'

Jim frowned. 'You've discussed my relationship with Jess with this guy?'

Adam didn't like the manner in which Jim's thumb had jerked in his direction. A man should be careful where he pointed his thumb. Especially if it brought him one step closer to Adam finding an excuse to swing for him.

'No, I haven't—'

'Because I'd really rather you didn't discuss my private matters with your new boyfriend.' The man attempted a smile. 'After all, who knows how long he'll stick around?'

Adam's hand bunched into a fist against his side. That was the second step. It would only really take one more...

Dana felt the tension in his body, so close against her own, and a glance confirmed her belief that his temper levels were rising. She reached an arm around his waist and searched down his arm until she found the fist. Then she began to pry it open with her smaller fingers, turning to press against his side as she did so.

She tilted her head and smiled a forced smile up at him. 'You planning on sticking around, *babes*?'

With a sideways glance at the other man, Adam smiled down into Dana's face. 'It would appear I am.' With those softly spoken words he studied her eyes intently. Then he surprised them both by leaning down and brushing his mouth across hers in a slow motion. 'I already said I was.'

Then he looked back at Jim. 'But how much time you

spend with Jim here knocking around is entirely up to you and Jess. Nothing to do with me.' He smiled one of his more potent smiles. 'I'll see you tomorrow.'

Dana blinked at him as he pulled free. She then stared in amazement as he leaned towards Jim's ear and said, 'I'll be here a lot. So I guess *you'll* be seeing me again too.'

And with that he winked at her over his shoulder and sauntered down the pathway. *Whistling*, for crying out loud.

# CHAPTER SIX

HIS mobile rang as he pulled into the car park of the riverside apartment block he lived in. With a glance at the screen he smiled and hit 'answer'. 'Hey, babes, miss me?'

Her voice echoed around the car's interior from the hands-free speaker. 'You ever call me babes again and I swear I'll kill you with my bare hands.'

He could think of other things he knew she was better at with her bare hands...

'Fine. What would you prefer, then? Sweetie, honey, hon? Whatever works for you when we're doing the ''in your face'' thing.'

There was a moment of silence at the end of the line. 'And that's what you were doing?'

'What else did you think it was?'

The silence returned again and Adam silently prayed she hadn't noticed his sudden bout of possessiveness. No, he *didn't* need the person setting the trap to know he'd felt its presence. Or that feeling its presence had actually been the first thing to really scare him since his cousin had told him monsters lived under the stairs. But then, he'd been four back then. That kind of information could change a boy's life.

'I wasn't aware we were still doing it.'

He pointed out an obvious fact. 'You played along.'

She hadn't exactly been sure what she was playing along with, and for a moment she'd liked the fact that he'd seemed a tad possessive over her. How many of these positive thoughts about Adam could she honestly keep blaming on raging hormones?

'Yes, I guess I did. But…at some point I'm going to have to tell him I'm pregnant.'

'Why, exactly?' It wasn't any of his damn business, was it?

'Because he might notice eventually?'

Okay. That made sense. 'When do you want to tell him?'

Adam wanted to be there when she did. Standing beside her through all this was becoming a more important thing to him each day.

She breathed deep for a moment or two. When she replied her voice was smaller. 'I'll wait a while. Until everything settles.'

Until she was sure she wouldn't lose the baby? He could almost hear the fear in her voice, and it created a bubble of fear in the pit of his own stomach. He didn't want her to lose this baby. He'd never even contemplated the idea of having one, but now he knew he didn't want to lose it. He took a small breath. 'Jack told me.'

'Told you what?'

'About the ones you lost.'

'You talked to him about my being pregnant?'

He laughed slightly. 'Hell, no. That's a fight waiting to happen.'

'So, what? He just volunteered the information?' Her voice grew angry. '"Isn't the weather great, Adam? Watch the match, Adam? Oh, and by the way, my sister had miscarriages and I just thought you should know in case you ever get her pregnant, *Adam*?"'

'No.' He frowned at her tone. 'It wasn't like that. I asked him about Tara being pregnant and we kind of worked our way round to it. But *you* should have told me.'

Yet another pause. 'And that's why you're wandering around doing the whole protective thing?'

His breath caught at the question. Was it? 'Partly.'

'And the rest of the reason is just because it irritates me?'

Anger surfaced as a mirror to the anger being thrown in his direction. 'No, actually, it's because I have this sudden and uninvited need to look after you. Apparently.'

'It's called guilt.'

'It's called assuming responsibility.'

'Who are you kidding? You can't even spell responsibility.'

Adam rolled his eyes heavenwards. 'I may not be husband material, but I intend making a damn good effort at being a good father. If you'll just let me try.'

'Why? You can't honestly tell me you wanted this to happen.'

He heard the tremor in her voice. Women were supposed to get emotional when they got pregnant, weren't they? Was that a good thing to happen, considering her history?

He started the engine up again. 'Neither of us planned this.' Making his voice as soothing as possible, he turned the car back out of the car park. 'But it's here now. Which means we're both going to have to bend a little for it to work out. We're both grown-ups; we can cope.'

Well, *one* of them was an adult, Dana thought. 'Unless I lose this baby.'

The tremor was more audible this time, and Adam sped up the road. 'I won't let that happen.'

Her breath caught. 'You can't control it.' She took a

shaky breath. 'It's me, you see. It's something wrong with me. It has to be.'

'Says who?'

Said Jim, as it happened. Both times. He'd told her there was obviously something wrong with her because she couldn't carry another baby full term. But then Jim hadn't wanted another baby. Dana had. Because she could love a baby unconditionally. What she'd thought she'd felt for her husband hadn't been enough to fill the void. But her daughter had proved a joy she couldn't have measured. She was a good mother, and with each child she would try to be the kind of mother she'd never had herself. But even that had been taken from her, time after time. Why would this time be any different?

'But it could be.'

Adam's voice was firm. 'Dana, it's not you, so you can stop that right now. There could have been a dozen reasons why, but at the end of the day it comes down to the fact that those children maybe just weren't supposed to be here.'

His soft, determined words tore at her heart, unleashing a small sob in her voice at her end of the line. 'And you think this one is?'

He smiled as he turned off the main road. 'You think this baby managed to make its way past that ninety-eight per cent barrier without good reason? Babes, this baby is damned determined to get here.'

Dana sniffed, but he could almost hear her smile. 'There you go, being nice to me again. I don't think you should do that when I'm hormonal and all. It's not safe.'

He laughed. 'Because you'll cry all over my designer shirts?'

'No.' There was a short pause. 'Because I might actually start to like you some, and I promised myself I wouldn't do that.'

The confession brought a smile to his mouth. Turning onto another smaller road, he parked the car and pulled the phone from the hands-free connector to tuck it against his ear. 'You already like me. It just kills you that you do.' He paused, got out of the car, and took a big step. 'And I don't think you're all that bad.'

'You hide it well.'

He walked forward and knocked on the door. When she opened it her phone was still pinned to her ear.

Adam smiled down at her shimmering eyes. He turned his phone off and tucked it into his pocket, then reached out to fold her hand in his and lead her back inside. 'We're going to get through this, Dana. Trust me. I won't abandon this child, and I'll be here with you all the way.'

Her throat closed off any words as her hormones went berserk. He said all the right things. That *damned* charm of his. Thing was, he'd said all the right things about being there for the baby, trying to be a good father and supporting her through the pregnancy, but he'd left out the one thing that would have made it even better.

He liked her. That was more than she'd expected. But Dana's mothering instincts wanted something more. She wanted this baby to have parents who loved each other. Because her own hadn't. And, as it turned out, Jess's hadn't. This time should have been different. If it had just been someone else...

'It'll be okay, Dana.'

He pulled her in against the haven of his strong body and stroked her hair when she eventually let go and sobbed. Adam Donovan was there for his baby. That was all. Dana knew that. It was simply that her hormones made her weep for the fact that, just once in her life, she would have quite liked the whole package.

Adam was beginning to realise there *was* a different world. He'd seen things on TV about alternate realities and parallel universes but they'd always been a tad too confusing. He understood better now.

He stood in the shop and stared around at the array of equipment. Baby stores were truly amazing places. Who'd have thought something so tiny as a baby could need so much *stuff*? And how did people ever afford to have more than one when everything cost so much?

Not that Adam was exactly strapped for cash. In fact he was financially more than secure, thanks to a favourite spinster aunt, his father's knack for investment portfolios and a successful business. But, hell, if the prices for small-baby stuff were any indication of how expenses would escalate as the child grew, he was going to have to think seriously about cashing in on some of his investments.

Wandering along the aisles, he started picking up the odd item—until he found his arms full and had to find a trolley to place them in. After half an hour one assistant pointed out to him that everything he had was for a boy, so he went back around the store and ended up buying an equal amount of girl stuff. In his mind he reasoned that with Tara pregnant too he stood a fairly good chance of finding a use for most of the items.

With his trolley already overflowing with bears, mini-football kits and other such essential items, he eventually stumbled across a set of bookshelves. Books on parenting screamed at him from every height. After a moment or two of frowning and blinking, he began flicking through them.

'Adam?' a female voice sounded. 'Adam *Donovan*?'

He turned and looked at the blonde-haired woman. He blinked as he tried to place a name on the face.

'It *is* you.' She smiled. 'Well, if ever there was someone I didn't expect to see in a baby store it was you!'

He willed his mind to recognise her, and then his eyes widened as the penny dropped. 'Gillian?'

His mother's best friend's daughter smiled back. 'Well done you for remembering me. After those couple of dates our mothers fixed us up on, I guess we both did our best to forget.'

Adam managed a smile. His mother had been relentless on the subject. But then his mother had been relentless on the subject of a steady girlfriend for him ever since he'd left home. As the only child it was his duty to find a nice girl, get married, and produce grandchildren for her to spoil. Oh, well, he could tick one off that list now. Yay him.

He smiled a genuine smile at her. 'It's been a while.'

She grinned and turned her profile to him to pat at her huge stomach. 'Yes—two of these ago.'

Adam stared, fascinated by her shape. Dana would be that shape, wouldn't she? All round and lush with the baby they'd made. He frowned a little at how arousing that thought suddenly was to him.

'Congratulations.'

She turned back and focused her attention on his trolley. 'You're buying a lot.'

He glanced down. 'There's a lot of stuff in this store.'

Gillian smiled. 'First time in a baby store, huh?'

With a glance from beneath his fringe, he grinned and nodded. 'Hell, yes.'

'So who's the lucky baby?'

The sales assistant he'd asked for help earlier returned with the brochures he'd requested. 'Mr Donovan? Hi. Our

manager says that we do hold this range of nursery furniture in the central warehouse. If your baby is due in
seven months then you would have time enough placing
the order in about five months.'

Adam accepted the proffered paperwork and smiled.
'Thanks.'

'*Your* baby?'

Oh-oh. He'd forgotten he had an audience. He pan-
icked, searching his mind eagerly for a convincing lie.

The helpful shop assistant grinned. 'Isn't it lovely? We
get a lot of first-time fathers spending a fortune with us.
I think they quite enjoy it.'

Gillian raised an eyebrow as she smiled back at the
young woman. 'I think they do too. My husband Kevin
spent a fortune with you when we had our first.' She
turned her attention back to Adam as the assistant smiled
her way down the aisle. 'Mother didn't mention you'd got
married.'

'I haven't.' He felt a flush touch his cheeks. 'This
just—'

She held up her hand. 'Oh, I don't need to know. Don't
worry. I think it's great you're taking such an active interest, though. I never would have seen you as the father
type.'

His green eyes narrowed at her words. Why was it that
everyone had that reaction? It was really starting to annoy
him.

'Did *you* know what it was like to be a mother before
you were one?' The words escaped before his brain had
assessed exactly what offence he might be causing.

Her eyes widened momentarily at his words, then a
smile appeared. 'No, I didn't. I'm sorry. I didn't mean it
as an insult, Adam.'

He shook his head. 'It doesn't matter.'

'No.' She reached out a hand and squeezed his upper arm. 'It does. You'll be fine, you know. Parenting is the toughest but most rewarding work you'll ever do in your entire life. And we both know what a workaholic you can be.'

His smile was genuine. He glanced down at his overflowing trolley, and then back up into her face. There was going to have to be an explanation here, and he knew it. If his mother was going to hear the glad tidings from anyone it should be him. Certainly not over coffee with her friends or at the amateur dramatic society...

'Look, Gillian—'

'Gillian, we're off now,' another female voice sounded from the end of the store.

Gillian waved, and then reached to squeeze Adam's arm again. 'It's been lovely bumping into you, Adam, and so good to see you taking this fatherhood thing seriously.' She raised an eyebrow. 'Many a bachelor doesn't, you know.'

He opened his mouth to continue, but she spun on her heel and walked briskly away. 'I'll see you at your parents' party anyway. Bye, Adam.'

'Gillian—?'

She waved over her shoulder without looking back. 'Byee!'

Adam gaped at her departing figure. Now he had another dilemma. He had to tell his mother before Friday that she was going to be a grandparent. His forehead creased into a frown. By Friday. Okay. He had some time to word it right. After all, it was only Monday. He just needed to work himself up to it a little. Maybe introduce her to Dana first.

He frowned harder as he looked back at the shelves.

Hell. One step at a time. First he needed to educate

himself. Then he could tell his mother—when he had all the information. It made sense. He had three and a half days. That was plenty of time.

In a way, it was vaguely ironic. But the atmosphere in their working environment *had* actually taken a turn for the better. Not a silly grinning, ridiculously polite atmosphere, but it had had a definite upgrade to occasional teasing, the odd genuine smile and rather a large portion of Adam-consideration in the atmosphere. It knocked people off their stride a little.

Especially Jack, who was spending a rare day inside the office. Usually he was out and about, finding sites and checking standards of workmanship. He designed at home, spoke to crews and customers on site, but when there came a time for hands to get dirty Jack relished the opportunity. Office visits were a rarity.

It meant that on the very occasional times he did visit the office he noticed changes. New pot plant, one of Dana's new filing systems, the fact that Adam kept glancing at Dana any time she moved anywhere…

'So, the foundations are in for the Johnston place, and the Lamont house is through Planning.'

'Mmm-hmm.' Adam glanced up as Dana walked back from the front reception area. She set coffees on the desks in front of them and he smiled up at her. She smiled a small smile back at him.

Jack leaned back, folded his arms across his chest and demanded, 'Okay, what's going on?'

Dana blinked at her brother. 'I made coffee.'

Adam glanced backwards and forwards, remaining silent as Jack thought, then said, 'No, not that. You two are being weird. What's going on?'

Adam glanced up at Dana's impassive face. She'd be hell to beat at poker. 'Nothing going on here, old pal.'

Jack snorted slightly. 'Sure there's not.'

'What would be going on?' Dana asked with questioning eyes.

Adam's eyes locked with hers. Ah. He could see it now. A spark of something in the depths of blue. Maybe he could beat her at poker after all. 'Maybe he should be more specific.'

Dana nodded. 'That would certainly help.' She tilted her head back in Jack's direction. 'You unhappy with something in the revised plans?'

He shook his head. 'Since when did you two start being civil to each other?'

His sister shrugged. 'We don't snipe at each other twenty-four hours a day. You've just happened to catch us at a good time, that's all.'

Blue eyes the exact match of her own narrowed slightly. But Dana held her ground. 'Maybe we decided it would be more productive if we tried being civil occasionally.'

Productive. *Mmm.* Adam tapped his chin with a long forefinger. Now, there was a word... He swivelled his chair in Jack's direction and smiled. 'Better working environment, don't ya know?'

'And now you're siding with each other *against* me.' Jack's face took on an expression of concern. 'Are we having financial difficulties? Did someone's house fall down and they're suing? What?'

Adam dropped his chin to his chest and pursed his lips to cover a smile at Jack's reasoning. He'd never imagined that being on Dana's team might be fun. It was just a shame he had to find out by lying to his best pal.

Dana merely smiled. 'Now you're panicking for no reason. There's nothing wrong with the business; no one is suing us. We've just called a truce.'

Jack seemed to think for a moment, frowned, then shrugged. 'Okay, fine. You two play whatever mind-games you're currently employing to torture each other with. Just leave the office standing when you're done.'

Adam gave a small guilt-filled smile as he looked up. 'We'll try.'

Dana studied Adam's expression. She could see the regret on his face at lying to Jack. Could see it because she felt it herself. Empathy, she surmised. That was all.

Jack turned his attention back to the plans in front of him. He lifted his coffee cup and glanced over at Adam. 'Tara said Friday was fine, by the way.'

Adam nodded. 'Great.'

Dana wondered what Friday was. She tried her best to not show she was interested, instead sitting down at her desk and turning her attention back to the material samples she was going through.

Adam studied her bowed head with a slight grin. He knew her curiosity was sparked. He was actually getting much better at reading her than he had been before. He didn't know why or how—but, hey, it was a useful addition.

She took a sigh-like breath as she moved her samples about. Eventually she glanced up and her eyes locked with his. She blinked a couple of times, then glanced across at her brother and back at Adam. *'What?'* she mouthed at him.

Adam glanced at Jack, then mouthed back, *'Nothing.'*

Dana's head tilted with a look on her face that said she didn't actually believe that. She glanced across and back. *'Really?'*

He grinned, shuffled a few forms together, and pushed his chair back.

Dana watched with cautious hooded eyes as he walked across the room and sat on the edge of her desk. He took a pen and pointed at the forms. 'Can you just check that Part C is relevant for the Murphy place?'

She narrowed her eyes and looked down at the form. On top was a piece of paper. Nice paper. It was an invitation to Mr and Mrs George Donovan's fortieth wedding anniversary party. On Friday night.

With a glance across at Jack's bowed head, she looked at Adam's slightly raised eyebrow.

'Well?' he demanded.

Her eyes widened. Another quick glance, and she swivelled her chair back and forth slightly as she pointed her pen at her chest. *'Me?'*

He nodded.

She swivelled again as she checked Jack. The pen pointed at Adam. *'With you?'*

He nodded again.

She laughed a little. Only it came out louder than intended.

Jack glanced up and she smiled. 'Adam's spelling is worse than Jess's.'

Jack shook his head and went back to work again.

Adam waited a moment, then glanced across at Jack and back at Dana. *'Well?'*

She watched his firm mouth form the word and found herself twisting her pen between her fingers as memories of that mouth invaded her mind. Apart from the most obvious reminder, she was having a lot of difficulty removing that one night from her memory. She ran the tip of her tongue across her mouth as she looked up into his eyes, and felt a jolt rock her stomach as he watched the movement, his pupils enlarging. Her heart beat a little louder as he looked back at her eyes. She shook her head.

Adam frowned at her rejection.

She raised an eyebrow in challenge and pushed the paper back towards him. Oh, she'd just bet he wasn't used to rejection. Well, tough.

'Okay. Not just the spelling, though, is it?' He spoke a little louder for Jack's benefit. 'I think I worded it wrong. Maybe if I worded it like this?' He wrote a few words on the back of the invitation and pushed it back across the desk.

Dana sighed quietly as she pulled her chair closer to the desk and read his scrawled words: *Why not? Too chicken?*

Her mouth dropped open in surprise. With a small glare upwards she scribbled over his words as she said, 'No, that wouldn't be it.' She wrote beneath the scribble: *I don't want to.*

Adam had read the words before they even made it back across the desk to him. 'Okay. Maybe this?'

The sheet came back. *Would one night kill you?*

Dana read the words and glared up at him as she wrote her answer: *Look what it did last time!*

'You really don't think sometimes, do you?' She shoved the sheet towards him and stood up.

'Ah.' Jack grinned down at a set of plans, his gaze not leaving them. 'Now, that's more like the conversation I'm used to in here.'

'And *you* have at least five more of those to look at before you see daylight again, so maybe you'd better just concentrate on what *you're* doing.' She threw the words over her shoulder as she walked out of the office and back into the main reception area.

Adam frowned from the corner of her desk as the door

closed. His eyes moved across to meet Jack's. 'Have I ever mentioned how much I owe you for sending her into this office?'

Jack grimaced. 'A time or two. But, hell, you liked her when you first met her.'

Adam shook his head. 'That was a long time ago—and before I got to know her. Now she's irritating as hell.'

'What did you do this time?'

A flush grew beneath the collar of Adam's shirt. Ah, now, there was a question.

'I'll be back in a minute. If I'm not, send for an ambulance.'

Jack grinned. 'For which one of you?'

She was tidying their receptionist's desk when he appeared.

'Deirdre hates it when you do that.'

'I know.'

'Then why do you do it?'

'Because it needs to be done.' She avoided his gaze and put pens into their holder.

Adam walked round behind her and turned her to face him with large hands on her shoulders. 'I want you to go with me.'

Dana blinked up at him. 'Why?'

'Because I think it would be a good idea if my parents got to meet the mother of their first grandchild.'

'I'm not good with people's parents.'

He frowned at her low words. 'What does that mean?'

'It doesn't matter what it means, Adam. I'm not going.' She tried to shrug out of his hands, her eyes darting back towards the office door. 'Really, I'm not.'

Adam's hands tightened, but his thumbs began a rough caress across her rounded shoulders. 'It's important.'

She looked back at his face, searched his eyes. Finding

only open sincerity caught her off guard, and she blinked again before answering with a whispered, 'Why?'

He took a breath and continued to massage her shoulders. 'Because when we have this baby I want my parents to be a big part of its life, like they were with mine and still are. And as you're the *mummy*—' he smiled at his use of the word '—they're going to want to get to know you too.'

Dana felt herself once again mesmerised by his words. It was amazing, the transformation he went through when he changed the tone of his voice to that low, hypnotic whisper, and when he used the distracting touch of his hands against her. She suddenly felt warm.

Her mind focused on a set of loving grandparents for her unborn child. Jim's parents had shown very little interest in Jess—not doted over her as they should have done, in Dana's opinion, and as Dana's own father did. It would be wrong to deprive this new child of that. What could it hurt to just find out what they were like? Just a peek. She could make up her mind later. It wasn't as if Adam was planning on telling them soon, or anything, right?

She swallowed to moisten her dry mouth. 'I'll think about it. But it's not a date.'

He smiled slowly. 'Why? Scared you might give in to temptation again?'

Her chin rose. 'Are you?'

His hands moved down her arms, drawing her closer to him. 'Not like there'd be any risk this time, would there?'

She swallowed again. 'That's true.'

His head tilted slightly and he looked at her mouth with hooded eyes. 'Not like we don't know now that we're compatible.'

Another jolt passed through her as her breasts hit the wall of his chest. 'Ironically, that's also true.'

His green eyes locked with hers. 'Have you thought about it?'

'That night?'

'Yes.'

She looked up at him as his head moved down towards hers, closed her eyes as his breath fanned across her face. The word came out in a whispered sigh. 'Yes.'

'Okay!' yelled Jack. 'I'm calling an ambulance in here!'

# CHAPTER SEVEN

MAYBE he really was some kind of pervert after all.

Adam scowled hard as he drove towards Dana's house. The house that, as it turned out, was so much closer to his than he'd ever realised before 'getting to know her'.

But, realistically, what other reason could there possibly be for this sudden fierce attraction he was experiencing for a pregnant female?

The simple truth was that it wasn't just any old pregnant female. It was Dana Taylor. Dana Taylor of the many faces—faces he was discovering on a daily basis. It was all rather a lot to take in.

Under normal circumstances he'd have gone and talked to Jack about the whole thing. A man-to-man talk to make sense of all things female. It was what they'd always done before—in a roundabout, football-analogies-used kind of way. But this time he was on his own—on his own at the one point in his life when he could really have done with some sensible advice.

His frown turned to a small smile at the irony in that statement. He was going to seek sensible advice from Jack? Jack, the best friend who had given up the bachelor lifestyle in favour of home and hearth? Oh, yeah, he could just imagine how advice from him would help. And as to the other football-cum-drinking buddies he had? Once they'd finished laughing they'd tell him to run like hell...

It wasn't that Adam was some kind of rebel, refusing to conform to the ways of society by avoiding relationships or a commitment to another human being. Hell, no.

He had everything in place, didn't he? He had a career and a good income and he owned his own home. He was a well-rounded guy. He simply had no desire whatsoever to go out and get settled with a woman just yet. Wasn't that a normal thing?

Well, not for most of the guys he knew the same age as him, it wasn't. 'You just haven't met the right woman yet.' That was the line normally aimed at him from varying directions—most of them female, it had to be said. A way for others to explain why he was still single, he guessed. And maybe it was true. He'd never felt so strongly about a female that he couldn't imagine his life without her in it. There had never even been the vaguest pull in that direction before.

Well, that wasn't strictly true, he admitted. There had been that one time, when he'd felt a tug so strong... But she'd had no interest in him, despite his fascination with her, so there hadn't been a thing he could do about it. He'd just had to get over it. So he had. Several times, actually.

But now there was this thing he had developed with Dana. Beyond being parents together, there was a something there—something new that he couldn't explain or reason away. It was making him crazy. And as for Dana— hell, the woman changed moods like the weather!

Add to all that the fact that it was now Thursday, and he hadn't spoken to his family yet, and life was just great. A bus could run over him any second now and he'd be fine with it.


'You're *what*?'

Dana grimaced slightly at Jim's tone. She was honestly beginning to believe that those two words should be used universally as some kind of catchphrase for pregnant women. There had been no right time to tell her ex-husband, so she'd just gone with the 'in with both feet' method.

The night before she'd sat down and broached the subject with Jess. Like all typical ten-year-olds, she had been both curious and stoic in her response to the whole thing. Despite Dana's nervousness Jess had been open to the idea of impending elder sibling-hood, and even a little enthusiastic at the idea of Adam being around more.

'I think he's okay.' That was praise indeed from someone her age.

Dana raised an eyebrow in suspicion. 'You do?'

Jess nodded across the sofa. 'Yeah. He's funny, and it's nice that he does stuff around the house.' She shrugged. 'It's more than Dad does. *And* he doesn't talk to me like I'm some dumb little kid.'

They continued watching the television for a while before Dana asked, 'It doesn't bug you that there'll be a baby around?'

Jess shrugged again. 'Nah. Some of my friends have babies in their houses and they're okay.' She looked at her mother with questioning eyes. 'You know they cry a lot, though?'

Dana smiled. 'I can remember.'

The minutes stretched out as they ate popcorn and watched the movie, then, 'Mum?'

'Yes?'

'Will Adam be moving in?'

Dana stared at her in shock. Would he *what*? 'I don't think so. We can manage, can't we?'

'We have before. But we didn't have a baby then.'

'That's true.' She searched for reassuring words. 'But we make a pretty good team, and I'm sure the family will help out.'

Jess ate popcorn for another moment. 'Well, just so you know, it's okay with me if you have a boyfriend. Dad has a girlfriend, and that's fine, so there wouldn't be a problem with you having a boyfriend.'

Sometimes her daughter's maturity took her by surprise. Child of the era of divorce, she guessed, which made her sad. She herself had been equally mature by that age, hadn't she? Out of necessity. Now she was parent to a mini-grown-up, and yet she wasn't mature enough to deal with how she felt about having Adam Donovan's baby. Life was just full to the brim of contradictions, really.

She sighed. 'Thanks, kiddo.'

Another shrug. 'No problem.'

Jim, however, was being less mature about it.

'How the hell could you be so stupid?'

Not that she hadn't asked the same question initially…but still. 'No, really—don't congratulate me, Jim.'

'What is there to congratulate?' He frowned across the kitchen at her. 'Are you going to marry that guy?'

'No.'

'Well, then, why in holy hell are you having a baby with him?'

'It wasn't exactly something we planned.' She frowned at her own use of the word 'we'. 'But it's a fact now, so there's no getting round it.'

'You can just get rid of it.' He folded his arms across his broad chest.

Her anger rose like a wave in her chest. It would be like taking away a part of her soul now. The life inside her was so real, no matter how tiny in actuality. 'I'm not getting rid of it. I'm keeping it.'

He laughed, a cruel sound that Dana remembered only

too well from the end of their marriage. It sent a chill of memory up her spine.

'What am I worried about? You'll probably not carry full term anyway, with your history. So why are you telling me?'

Her face paled at his words and she gripped the back of the wooden chair in front of her until her knuckles turned white. 'I'm telling you out of simple courtesy. I thought it better you heard it from me than from Jess.'

'You told Jess?' His voice rose. 'How could you do that?'

'Because she needs to know, for crying out loud!'

'Not if you lose it, she doesn't!'

*Son of a—* She took a deep breath and tried to remain calm.

Stress was not a good thing. She had to remember that.

'I told her because I talk to her about everything that might have an impact on her life—because that's what a parent should do when their child is old enough to understand what's going on around them! I won't have her worry or feel insecure because of anything I do. It's that simple.' She shook her head. 'Not that you'd understand that.'

His fair head tilted to one side and he studied her with hazel eyes. 'Meaning that you're a more responsible parent than me? Is that what you're saying?'

She sighed and ran a hand across her forehead. Her voice sounded weary, even to her own ears. 'I'm not trying to start another argument with you, no matter what you may think. I'm just being honest with you—which is all I've ever tried to be. I'm pregnant. It's not a big, complicated thing. And I'm having this baby.'

*'Maybe.'*

His jibe struck home at a deep level. 'Go away, Jim. I've told you now. It wasn't meant to be a discussion.'

'Well, I think it needs to be discussed!' His face grew red with anger.

'Go away.' She pulled out the chair and sat down at the worn oak table, her eyes devoid of emotion as she looked up at him. 'You gave up any right to any discussion of my life when you made the decision to walk out.'

'I didn't give up the right to discuss things that affect my daughter's life.'

'So we should have discussed you and Melanie, then, should we?' She smiled sarcastically. 'Or maybe the half-dozen there were before that? You're such a hypocrite.'

He shook his head. 'I don't even know why I bother talking to you any more. We always end up in an argument.'

'Yes, we do.' That was how they'd known in the end that they just didn't work as a couple. They'd probably known for a long time. But Jim had been too much of a coward to admit it and Dana had been too determined to stand by the choices she'd made. She wasn't going to make the same mistakes as the generation before her. Her child was going to be raised in a happy home. The mistake still hurt. 'And that's why we're better apart. I stay out of your life with Melanie, despite how much you try to rub my face in it.'

'Oh, and bringing that guy to the reunion wasn't rubbing *my* face in it?'

She avoided his eyes as he asked the question. She'd just been so determined to be doing as well as him. It had been her stupid pride. Well, they did say pride came before something. She just hadn't quite expected the something that the something had turned out to be.

A thought occurred to her. 'Is that why you've suddenly decided to see so much of Jess?'

'If that man is going to be a part of my daughter's life I have a right to know what sort of guy he is.'

She ran her hand across her forehead again. 'Fine, then take him to a football match or something. But just try minding your own business when it comes to me and my relationship with him.' Her head pounded.

'Fine.'

'Good.'

'Yeah, right.' He shook his head again. 'You just love screwing up your life, don't you, Dana?' He smiled a cruel smile. 'Good luck with the baby. You'll need it.'

Dana stared at the doorway for a long time after he'd gone through it. It took a while before she actually noticed she was crying. Silent, pain-filled tears ran down over her cheeks and splashed onto the table top. He was right. Damn him, but he was right. She really did make a career out of screwing up her life.

Adam was unprepared for the face that greeted him when Dana's door swung open. He frowned and stepped over the threshold, gripping her forearms with his large hands. 'What's wrong?'

Dana blinked up at the concern in his green eyes and tried her best for a blank expression. 'Nothing. I'm fine.'

'Liar.'

She allowed him to turn her around and steer her towards the living room. 'Really, Adam, I'm fine.'

'Let's just see, shall we?' Turning her again, he tilted his head to make a closer study of her eyes. He smiled gently and spoke in a soft voice. *'Liar.'*

'Sometimes I really, truly don't like you, you know.' She huffed a little as she sat down on the sofa.

'Yeah, I know.' He continued smiling. 'Stay there.'

She watched with guarded eyes as he left the room, returning long minutes later with two mugs. He handed one to her before pulling the coffee table closer to where she sat, her legs curled beneath her. 'Where's Jess?'

'My sister Lauren's.'

'Okay.' He tilted the mug to his mouth and asked her over the rim, 'So, what's up?'

She frowned and pursed her lips slightly. 'Oh, and now you're what? Uncle Adam? Why in the name of hell would I want to tell *you*?'

'Anyone ever mention how prickly you can be sometimes?'

'Maybe I have cause to be.' She hid her face in her mug as the words spilled out. It was really getting to the stage where she was in need of a gag when Adam was around.

'Why?'

She glanced up at his face, her eyes travelling over his disobedient fringe before they met with the sincerity in the green depths of his thick-lashed eyes. 'Why do you want to know?'

His eyes sparkled slightly. 'Damned if I know.'

An eyebrow raised. 'Now who's the liar?'

He moved his mug in small circles between his large hands, studying its steaming contents before his eyes rose to meet hers again. 'Okay, why don't we both take a chance here, and try being completely honest with each other for the remainder of this conversation?'

Her breath caught in her chest at the suggestion. 'You think you can do that?'

His eyes challenged her. 'You think *you* can?'

They stared at each other while silence entered the

room. Dana searched his eyes again. 'What do you think it would achieve?'

Adam's wide shoulders raised in a shrug, stretching the material of his dark sweater across his chest. 'I believe it's called communication. Supposedly it's advisable between parents.'

Her blue eyes blinked at him.

Adam smiled, a dimple appearing in each of his cheeks. 'Hey, I'm not saying I'll find it any easier than you will, but it's worth a try. I'm a big guy—I'm up for the challenge.'

Her eyes narrowed slightly at his words, but his smile was infectious. Funny how she was understanding more every day about what all those other women saw in Adam Donovan. He did have his good points.

'You first.'

He laughed, the smile promoting itself to a grin and putting his straight white teeth on display. 'Somehow I knew you'd say that.'

Dana leaned her shoulders back against the well-stuffed cushions of the sofa and smiled back at him. 'I guess you can only work with someone for so long before you eventually start to get to know them.'

'We've managed not to, though, haven't we?'

She tilted her head a barely visible inch. 'Have we started the honesty thing now?'

He nodded.

She mirrored the movement. 'Yes, we've managed not to get to know each other—but that's maybe got something to do with the fact that we don't exactly get on.'

He considered her words, his eyes still on her face. 'Maybe because until the reunion night we'd never tried.'

She grimaced. 'Oh, yeah, and look where that got us.'

'All right, so that's not a good example.' The smile

remained. 'But maybe it was just easier for us to argue the whole time than it was to try actually talking to each other.'

Her heart thumped a loud beat against her ribs. She glanced away from his addictive smile and studied the contents of her mug intently. 'And why do you think that is?'

Adam thought his answer through carefully. 'Because isn't that what most people do? Hide behind something or other?'

She glanced up from beneath long lashes. 'You hide?'

His eyes searched the room for a second and he shrugged again. 'I guess.'

'Rather than make an attachment to someone?'

*Was* that what he did? The question caught him off guard, but after a moment's thought he realised that she was right. It was exactly what he did. Because he liked the uncomplicated simplicity of single life, liked the lack of attachments. He could go where he wanted to go, see who he wanted to see. He was free as a bird.

But as he looked back into Dana's too blue eyes and felt the newly familiar tug towards her, he wondered for the first time if it wasn't just the littlest bit lonely.

He shook his head at the thought.

She raised her eyebrow again. 'Is that a no?'

He managed a downward smile at the contents of his mug. 'No, it's not a no. I've just never thought about it that way. You're right.'

'Why?'

The low tone of her voice drew his attention back to her face. He watched as she tried to hide her eyes from him with a sip of her tea. He watched her small fingers curl around the mug, saw her throat move as she swallowed, and then her eyes looked back into his.

He blinked. 'I just never thought it was for me.'

She looked away again, unreasonably disappointed by his answer. But she'd known it already, really, hadn't she? So there was no surprise. She tried to hide behind a smile as she looked back at him.

'The everlasting bachelor, huh?'

'Something like that.'

She nodded and continued to smile.

After a moment Adam actually managed to look away from her face. It was quite an achievement, considering how gorgeous she looked. It *had* to be that pregnant glow he'd heard so much about. He cleared his throat. 'So, what about you?'

'You already told me. I'm prickly.'

'Because of Jim?' His eyes shot back to her face as the question jumped out.

She nodded before taking another sip of tea. 'Among other things, I guess.'

'Did he break your heart?'

Had he? She frowned for a moment as she thought about her answer, keeping her eyes lowered and hidden. It irritated her immensely when her voice shook on the words. 'When you love someone enough to marry them, you want it to work. You want them to love you as much as you try to love them. It's hard to let go of that. But I think the failure broke my heart more than anything else.'

Adam frowned inwardly at her words. He wondered if she still regretted that it hadn't worked. If there was a chance, would she try again?

He discovered his honesty only stretched so far, choosing to state the obvious instead. 'Because you like to be in control and it was taken from you?'

Her eyes shot to his. 'What did you do, Adam? Take a degree in psychobabble at some point so you can pinpoint

the reasons behind a prospective customer being defen
sive?'

His green eyes remained steady. 'Prickly.'

She glared at him.

'I'm right, aren't I?' He made his voice soothing, lean
ing his upper body a little closer as he spoke. 'It's why
you're so anally retentive at work, and in the way you
look outside of this house. You like to be in control
Because if you're in control you feel safe.'

She blinked and felt her eyes well up again.

He set his cup down beside him and held her gaze. 'Bu
here, inside this house, you get to be you. A little chaotic
more disorganised, and you let yourself look all soft and
feminine and relaxed. When someone walks through tha
front door it's like they're walking straight into a little
piece of you. You know that, right?'

She felt her heart beat faster at his words and nodded

He moved across the divide and sat on the sofa beside
her. 'And, since we're being honest, I have to confess I
like this you better—the one that's slightly less in control.'

She managed a small smile. 'As opposed to the one
that completely *lost* control on the reunion night?'

One large hand reached out and removed the cup from
her hand, setting it down on the table before he sat close
enough to touch his shoulder to hers. 'No.' His voice was
pure seduction. 'I kinda liked that one too.'

She watched, mesmerised, as he reached out to smooth
her hair from her cheek, warm fingertips trailing against
her skin. Her eyelids grew heavy. 'What are we doing
Adam?'

He took a deep breath. 'I haven't the faintest idea.'

The temptation to lean herself into his side was im-
mense. It would be so easy. She could just lean a little

bit and he would take the weight. She could feel his warmth beside her, could feel the hard strength of his body. For just a tiny moment she could lean. Just this once.

Adam felt her weight increase slightly against his side. Without thinking or reasoning or fighting the sensation he allowed his arm to snake around her slight shoulders and pull her closer. His other hand reached for her chin and tilted her head up so he could get lost in her eyes again.

She, in turn, dutifully raised those eyes and looked up at him, blinking slowly.

His chest grew tight. Good God, he was in trouble.

Her mouth curved into a slow smile. 'It's okay, Adam.' Her voice was soft, almost but not quite a whisper. 'I know this isn't anything to you. I just need to lean for a little minute, I guess. It's a moment of weakness; it'll go away. You don't have to kiss me or anything.'

He smiled a slow smile in reply, wondering if the fear had actually shown in his eyes. 'Are we still doing the honesty thing?'

She allowed her traitorous fingers to move up and smooth his thick fringe back from his forehead. 'Yep.'

It was suddenly amazing to him how that one movement, motherly in one way, could be so damned sexy in another. His hand turned, cupped her chin, his thumb moving up to touch the corner of her mouth. 'Thing is, Dana, I *want* to kiss you.'

As her mouth formed a silent 'oh' he leaned down and pressed his mouth to it. He waited a second for her to struggle or protest, but instead she moved her lips to fit his and let a little breath out. He smiled, then tilted his head and moved with her, slowly, softly. So different from the night they'd made love, when everything they'd done had been hot, heavy and desperate. It entered his mind how each time he kissed her he seemed to be kissing someone different. It was fascinating. It was sexy as hell.

She reached a hand up and placed it flat against his face, moving her thumb against his cheek. When she felt his thumb move at the corner of her mouth, so close to where their lips were joined, she automatically moved her thumb to the same place on his face. She mimicked his movements, echoed them like a reflection in a mirror.

Eventually his head raised and he looked down at her flushed face, his thumb remaining against the edge of her swollen lips. She opened her eyes and looked up at him. He swallowed hard. 'You need to tell me to stop now.'

She nodded slowly at the sense in his words. 'Yes, I do. Because there's no point. This isn't going anywhere.'

His thumb brushed across her lower lip. 'You're right.'

Her thumb echoed the movement and she watched it with dark eyes. 'Because we both lead very different lives.'

He nodded. 'Yes, we do.'

Her head tilted slightly towards his neck. 'The only thing we have in common is this baby.'

'Yes.'

'And work.'

He lowered his head towards her again. 'Uh-huh.'

'I know you're not interested in long-term attachment.'

'Correct.' He brushed his mouth across hers. 'And you're not interested in an affair with me because you hate losing control. Because your life is already complicated enough, with Jim in the picture.'

She repeated the small kiss. 'Maybe. But with you it would seem I do lose control.'

His body tightened at her words. Big, big, *big* trouble. Huge. The trap was closing in and he couldn't move away.

He turned the small kisses into something firmer and stronger and immediately felt the transformation. The other Dana appeared, the one from the reunion night. She pushed closer to him and moved her mouth hungrily, opening her lips to his searching tongue.

Adam groaned. Trouble.

The back door slammed with such force that the house almost shook. 'Mum—I'm home. Where are you? Is Adam here?'

They jumped apart like two teenagers discovered by parents. As Adam looked across at her he grinned, then whispered, 'You know, one of these days there's not going to *be* someone to interrupt us.'

Dana sent a silent prayer that she would find some common sense before that happened.

# CHAPTER EIGHT

'YOU look gorgeous.'

Dana smiled at Tara. 'Thank you—and ditto. You see?' She leaned forward to whisper. 'I *can* actually dress myself when I try.'

Tara laughed. 'So I see. But, really, you do look fantastic.' She smiled and narrowed her eyes slightly. 'There's something different, though. What is it?'

Dana had to force herself not to move a hand to her stomach. She knew it wasn't noticeable yet, and certainly not below the empire line evening dress she'd bought that morning. Nope, short of an actual test result she was a good few months away from being obvious just yet.

Her eyes glanced around the crowded room for a glimpse of a familiar fair head.

Tara smiled at her profile. 'He's with Jack at the buffet table.'

Dana's eyes skimmed across to the long table, located the two men, then skimmed onwards around the room. As if that was what she'd been meaning to do the entire time. She kept her voice nonchalant. 'Who?'

Laughter sounded from the general direction of her sister-in-law. 'Your date.'

Her head shot round to face Tara again. 'It's *not* a date.'

Tara shrugged. 'Whatever you want. But I'm just saying, you were looking for Adam and he's with Jack.'

'That's nice for him.'

'Adam or Jack?'

Dana sighed. 'Can we not play this right now?'

Tara's face was immediately apologetic at the look of sheer exhaustion that crossed Dana's face. She reached out and touched a hand to Dana's arm. 'Lord, I'm sorry, Dana. I didn't mean to annoy you. I live with your brother, remember? Verbal banter is a way of life in our house. I just forget sometimes.'

'Don't worry.' She glanced back across the room, frowned at the direction her curious eyes had led her in, then glanced back. 'I guess I'm just sensitive at the minute.' She grimaced slightly. 'Long story.'

Tara seemed to think about pursuing the conversation, then thought better of it. Instead, they both looked around the crowded room.

Then Tara glanced across from the corner of her eye. 'So, are you and Adam friends now?'

*Friends?* Dana blinked slowly as she let the word turn over in her mind. Was that what they were now? Could what they were even fit into a particular category? Somehow she doubted it.

'I guess you could say we're working at it.'

They looked around at the well-dressed people again, while a piano played from somewhere at the other end of the room.

Tara's line of thought continued. 'Can I ask you a question?'

Dana's breath caught. *Oh-oh.* She nodded silently.

'Has it ever occurred to you...?' She studied Dana's tense profile. 'Well... Because it's occurred to me—you know...'

Dana glanced at her. 'Go on, Tara, spit it out.' She clenched her hand a little tighter around her glass of lime and soda.

'Has it occurred to you that maybe part of the reason

you think you dislike Adam so much is because he re-
minds you a little of Jim?'

Of all the various questions her imagination had led her
to believe Tara might ask, this one was furthest down the
list. She turned to face her and frowned. 'What?'

Tara blushed slightly. 'Well, you have to admit they do
look very alike. Both tall, both fair-haired, both sort of
boyish-looking. It has struck me that maybe it's the main
reason you've been so hard on him.'

His usual irritating, arrogant personality and the way
he treated the women he dated wasn't enough reason?
Dana continued to gape.

'He's not that bad a guy once you get to know him,'
Tara went on. 'Okay, he's still very much the bachelor
type. The love 'em and leave 'em guy we were all warned
about by our parents. But he wouldn't be the first one of
those on the planet to soften when he met the right
woman.'

Dana shook her head. 'Where has all this come from?'

The blush grew deeper. 'We just thought that since you
two seem to be getting on so much better you must have
looked past your prejudices.'

'*We?*'

'So, what's going on with you and my sister?'

Adam almost choked on a piece of sausage. Dangerous
thing, a buffet table. He swallowed a mouthful of beer to
wash it down, and glanced at his friend through watery
eyes. 'What do you mean?'

Jack shrugged. 'Well, you've brought her to your
parents' party as your date, for starters.'

'It's not a date.' He kept his face as serious as possible
while looking Jack in the eye. Dana had told him five

times in the car on the way over that it wasn't a date. She'd been quite insistent about it, in fact.

Jack wore his disbelieving look—the look he normally wore when Adam suggested that his sports car wasn't expensive to run. 'Okay, so, what? You're friends or something now, then?'

Were they? Adam mulled over his definition of *friends* in his head and knew that they weren't that. Not when he couldn't spend any time in her immediate vicinity without thinking about kissing her or just plain holding her. The latter of which was the more dangerous, in his opinion. Friends? Nah. They went somewhat beyond that.

Which did rather invite the question—what were they?

He felt a flush begin at the neck of his shirt. Oh, great.

He managed a nonchalant shrug of his shoulders beneath his jacket. 'It's no big deal, Jack. We've just got to know each other a little better, that's all.'

*Got to know each other a little better?* Jack's eyebrows rose at the words. 'Oh, really?'

Someone should just go fetch him a shovel. 'Jack, are you asking me if there's anything going on between your sister and me?'

'As the only brother to four sisters, it's kind of my job to look out for their interests.'

'And I can only imagine how well that sits with Dana.'

'Maybe if I'd watched out better she might not have got hurt so badly last time.'

Adam frowned at his friend's words. He couldn't honestly be blaming himself for that, could he? 'She makes her own decisions.'

'Yes, she does.' Jack smiled wryly. 'But that doesn't stop me from hurting when she hurts, or trying in my own way to make sure she doesn't hurt like that again. It's called caring—it's what you do when someone means something.'

Adam nodded. 'Thanks for that insight. I'd obviously not have known that, having never cared for anyone my entire life.'

'I didn't mean that.'

'Didn't you?' His eyes travelled across the room to where Dana stood. 'It's what your sister has thought pretty much since she first clapped eyes on me.'

Jack studied Adam's profile. 'Mmm…Tara and I have a theory on that one.'

Green eyes locked with blue. 'And?'

'We think you remind her of Jim.'

'Thanks a bunch.' He reached out for his glass and turned to leave the table. Jack's hand on his arm held him back. He looked down at the hand until it released its grip, then looked back up into Jack's face. 'If I've got my facts right, that means you think I'm like a guy who ran out on his wife and kid and took up with another woman. It's nice to know that your opinion of me is nearly as high as your sister's.'

'That's not what I'm saying. You don't know the whole story.'

'Because no one has told me!'

Jack shrugged, feeling a pang of guilt at the information he'd already supplied about his sister. There was something going on; he could feel it. And knowing that brought out his protective streak. 'It's not our place to tell you. It's Dana's.'

'If she already thinks I'm like him then she's hardly likely to confide in me, is she?' It was amazing how much that thought twisted his gut. He wanted her to talk to him. It *mattered*.

'I don't even think she realises that's why she's so hard

on you—and, for the record, I *don't* think you're like him. You just *look* a bit like him, and I'm sure that's one of the first things she saw when she met you.'

His eyes found their way back to her again as the words tumbled around inside his head. Was that it? Was it really as simple as that?

The first time they'd met officially had been at some family do Jack had invited him to, and she'd been there, across the room, with her hair falling around her shoulders like a dark curtain. She'd been beautiful. Beautiful, with an air of almost unbearable sadness in her eyes. Adam had felt the pull of her from clean across the room, and yet when he'd been introduced she'd looked at him as if he was evil incarnate. It had put his back up, and thus their niggling dislike for each other had begun.

If it had been because he reminded her of Jim then it at least made some sense—became less personal, somehow. But at the same time he didn't want to remind her of her ex-husband. The man who'd run out on her. The man who hadn't cared enough to stick around. The one who somewhere deep inside she was maybe still in love with? Was that why it had hurt her so much?

Jack watched the thoughts run over his friend's face. He smiled a small smile. He recognised that look only too well. It hadn't been so long ago that he'd worn that same kind of confusion himself.

'So, should I be having a talk with you regarding your intentions?' He smiled as he asked the question, knowing his friend would take it with the humour he had meant. But the look in Adam's eyes when he looked back at him completely knocked him out.

'Jack—'

Jack held a hand in front of him. 'Hey, it was a joke

Adam—don't look so serious. I'm glad you two are getting along better, and it's really none of my business.'

Adam's eyebrows rose.

'Seriously, it's not.' He laughed. 'I'll just have to kill you if you hurt her, that's all.'

Adam took a deep breath and looked his friend directly in the eye. 'I would never do anything to deliberately hurt her.'

'Then that's fine with me.'

'You must be Dana.' The older woman engulfed her in a warm embrace. 'I can't tell you how much I've been looking forward to meeting you. You've made my anniversary for me.'

'I have?' Dana asked from mid-hug.

She could only assume from the brief glimpse she'd had of green eyes that the woman was Adam's mother. But why had she made her anniversary for her? Her eyes looked over the shoulder her chin rested on to Adam, as he pushed through the crowd towards her with a vague look of panic on his face.

The woman held her at arm's length to look at her. 'And aren't you just lovely? I always knew Adam would end up with some beautiful young thing. He just took his time about it, I guess.'

Dana smiled weakly.

A somewhat flushed Adam appeared between them, his eyes glancing from Dana to his mother and back. 'You two have met, then?'

'Not exactly.' Dana glared up at him, only vaguely aware that Jack had also appeared, with Tara at his side. 'Your mother was just saying how I've made her anniversary for her...?'

'She was?' He frowned in confusion as he looked down at her. He looked at his mother. 'She has?'

His mother continued to smile at Dana. 'I'm sorry, I should have at least introduced myself before I hugged you, shouldn't I?' She laughed. 'That's just typical of me. But I was so excited to meet you.'

Adam blinked at his mother. He'd always known she could be a little crazy, but... 'Dana—my mother Anne. Mother—you've met Dana, obviously.'

She swatted at his arm with a hand before linking her arm through his. 'Yes, and you should have brought her to meet me before now.' Her eyes flicked from Dana for a moment. 'Oh, hello, Jack, Tara.'

They both greeted her with hellos in stereo before continuing to watch the action in front of them unfold.

Dana smiled at Anne through gritted teeth.

Anne squeezed her son's arm, looking up at him as she scolded, 'I can't believe you were waiting until tonight to tell us. If Barbara hadn't spilled the beans days ago I'd never have known.' She smiled a genuinely warm smile at Dana. 'But, really, this is just the best gift. We're both so pleased for you.'

Everything suddenly made sense in Adam's head. He stared at his mother in dismay. Barbara. Gillian's mother Barbara. He nodded slightly. This was what happened when he didn't get round to talking with his mother before this evening. Because he'd kept on putting it off. He took a breath and looked at Dana, knowing he was deeply, deeply in trouble.

Her eyes locked with his. Despite the smile on her lips he knew he was a dead man. Well, this time it wasn't his fault. Entirely.

'Dana—'

'You brought me here tonight as an *anniversary present*?'

'No, I didn't!' He frowned down at her. 'I brought you here tonight as my—'

His words faltered as he looked around at his small audience. Aw, to hell with it. In for a penny and all that. He looked back into her eyes. *'Date.'*

She gasped. 'This is *not* a date. We agreed.'

'You've accompanied me to my parents' anniversary. We travelled here together, we'll spend the evening here together, and then I'll take you home. I may even kiss you goodnight—*if* you get lucky.' He smiled and continued, despite her widening eyes. 'That pretty much constitutes a date.'

Tara and Jack began to smile too. Dana positively growled up at him, and his mother stepped a little out from his side towards the growling person. 'I'm so sorry that Barbara ruined the surprise for you both.'

Adam turned to his mother. 'It's not exactly what you think. I should have come to see you earlier, but things have been...' He glanced back at Dana for a split second. 'Complicated.'

Dana finally put his words into order in her head. *'You* didn't tell your mother we were together?'

He shook his head, his voice low and intimate. *'No.'*

'Oh, no, my best friend's daughter bumped into him at the start of the week.'

Dana looked at Anne with a blank expression. 'Oh?'

Adam knew that 'oh' probably translated to his mother as an 'I understand'—when in actuality Dana still hadn't a clue what was going on, or that his mother knew about the baby. With a little swift footwork he could save this. They were going to have to tell Jack and Tara now. That was a given. But he wanted to tell them at Dana's side, presenting a united front. Not mid-argument.

But his mother was on a roll. She laughed musically. 'I think the fact that he was buying a lorryload of baby equipment gave it away.'

The air seemed to go still and quiet as the small group worked out the meaning behind her words.

Adam closed his eyes for a second, as if by shutting out the sight of everyone he could make the mess just go away. When he opened them he was immediately presented with several different emotions on several different faces. His mother looked as if Christmas had arrived, Tara looked stunned, Jack looked as if he might explode, and Dana...

As he looked into her eyes he felt lower than a snake's belly button. She looked stricken, devastated. He stepped towards her. She stepped back from him, her arms wrapping around her waist. 'You *bought* baby stuff?'

'Just a couple of things—'

'Half the store, from what I hear.' His mother tried to make it sound like a good thing as her eyes looked around with growing concern at the other faces. 'I thought it was the sweetest thing that he was having so much fun getting it all. Never thought I'd see the day...'

Adam only vaguely heard the words, and they gradually faded away. He stepped closer again and reached a hand towards Dana.

She shrugged away from his touch and glanced frantically around her, then back at his face. 'How could you *be* so stupid?' She hissed the words up at him.

'Dana—'

Jack stepped in to shield her from him, taking a deep breath which puffed his chest out. 'Not now, Adam.'

'Jack, let me talk to her.' From behind her human shield

Adam could see Dana being taken away by Tara. 'I just need a minute.'

'Oh, I think you've had plenty of opportunities for that minute.' Jack placed a hand flat against Adam's chest and stared him straight in the eye. 'With all of us.'

Adam pushed against Jack's hand. 'I need to see if she's okay.'

'We'll do that.'

Adam shook his head. 'No, I—'

'You what, Adam?' Jack pushed him back again as he asked questions in a low voice. 'Care about her? Love her? What?'

'Adam, what's going on?' his mother's voice demanded.

He looked across at her. 'Like I said, Mother, it's complicated.'

'I've put my foot in it again, haven't I?'

He smiled in reassurance. 'This isn't your fault. I should have done something to fix this before now.' A hand reached out to tap her arm. 'Go back to the party. I'll explain it all tomorrow. I promise. Don't worry.'

They both turned and smiled bright smiles at her, then waited until she had gone. Then, smile fading into nothing, Jack looked back into Adam's eyes. 'This is a bloody mess.'

'Like I just said, I should have sorted this before now.'

Jack nodded. 'Yes, you should.'

'We would have told you.'

He shrugged. 'I believe you.'

Adam looked across the room as Dana and Tara left. 'Let me talk to her, Jack.'

Jack moved to the side to block his way again. 'When you decide what it is you want, then you can talk to her.

For now, you leave her alone.' He leaned forward. 'Don't make me hit you, Adam.'

Adam was more than capable of defending himself, and they both knew it. He took a deep breath. He guessed he was due at least one good punch for all this.

'This is between your sister and me.'

Jack smiled sarcastically. 'It would have to have been, wouldn't it?'

'You won't keep me from her for long.'

Jack's suspicious eyes studied his friend for several long moments. 'Until you figure out just what the hell you want from her, and until that look of pain leaves her eyes, I'll move heaven and earth to keep you away from her.'

Adam stepped back, looking Jack straight in the eye. 'You're going to have to, Jack. Because that's what it'll take.'

'And again, I'll ask why?'

Adam's jaw clenched and unclenched as he stared into Jack's face.

Jack waited patiently, then shoved his hands into his pockets with a small, wry smile. 'That's what I thought.'

'You don't have the faintest idea how I feel about all this.' Adam's words were low and rough. He thought again how under normal circumstances it would have been Jack he'd have talked to. 'No one does.'

Jack nodded. 'Neither do you. And that's where your problem lies, isn't it?' With a glance over his shoulder he began to reverse a few steps. 'Give it some time, Adam. She has her family to look after her now. You take some time and think.' His eyes narrowed. 'Think *real* hard.'

Adam watched as he walked away, then watched the room for several long minutes. Then he thought about the reason he was in the room. A wave of guilt crossed him, and he went and searched for his mother. He could at least try and fix something. He smiled as his eyes met hers. He wouldn't be the one to ruin her party.

With a nod he walked over and held her in a huge hug. 'You all right?'

He nodded as he loosened his grip to look down at her. 'I'm fine.'

'You shouldn't lie to me, you know. I'm your mother. I have an instinct for these things. Even if I'm very, very poor at subtlety.'

'It's not your fault.' He shrugged. 'I messed up—big-time.'

'By getting her pregnant in the first place or by not talking about it?'

He took a breath. 'By not talking about it. I've got used to the first part a little, and I'm of the opinion that if something's meant to happen it's meant to happen.'

She leaned a little closer and looked up at him with soft eyes. 'Do you love her?'

'I don't exactly have a lot of experience with falling in love.'

'So, you don't know, then?'

He forced a grin. 'Couldn't you just go and enjoy your party like a good girl and stop worrying about me?'

She patted his cheek as if he was still ten. 'I never stop worrying about you. You're going to be a father. You'll understand.'

'I guess I will.'

Her perceptive eyes studied him for a second, then she stepped out of his arms. 'I'd better go and be a hostess again.' She continued watching as he nodded. 'Though I have to say it's interesting to me that it's Dana.'

Adam frowned. 'Why?'

'Because she's not anything like any of the women I've

heard you dated before. She's more like the type you were interested in before you went on your bachelor binge.'

The words raised a smile. 'My what?'

'Binge, darling.' She leaned her head in to speak quietly. 'For about five or six years now, I think. It's the funniest thing. Because you were never so insular before that.'

He leaned down and accepted the kiss she planted on his cheek.

She smiled up at him. 'Good luck, my darling. Do let me know how it turns out—so I don't have to hear it from Barbara.'

# CHAPTER NINE

THE door opened and a very rumpled Adam stood in front of her. She swallowed hard, her traitorous body warming at the sight of him. Damn, the man just *was* sex on legs, wasn't he?

He blinked at her with his green eyes, running his long fingers back through his fringe, which stuck out ridiculously in all directions. 'You're here.'

Dana nodded silently and let her eyes move down over his wrinkled grey T-shirt and dark jogging pants to his bare feet. She damped her lips and looked back up at his face. 'You and I need a talk.'

'I was coming to see you this morning.'

'You'd have had to get past Jack first.'

He smiled. 'I thought a night might have settled him a little.'

'Nope.'

With a glance at his watch he realised it was seven-thirty. 'Hell, Dana, what did you do? Break out over the wall at dawn or something?' He stepped back and allowed her to pass him before closing the door behind her. 'You must be exhausted.'

Dana's eyes glanced curiously around the interior of his apartment. So very different from her home. It was yet another example of the differences between them, she guessed. She walked over the smooth laminated floors to the full-length windows that looked out over the river below. Very chic.

Adam watched as she looked around his apartment. His

attempt at levity hadn't even broken her concentration, and he felt a sudden sense of foreboding. 'You want tea?'

She shook her head, running her hand along the back of the leather sofa as she walked around the room. 'No, thank you.'

'Something to eat?'

She glanced quickly at him, then away as she smiled a little. 'No, I've hit a throwing-up phase, so probably best I don't.'

Adam wondered how much of the throwing up was due to the baby and how much was due to the stress she was under.

She took a breath, stopping in front of a chair. 'Could we sit?'

He studied her face. The foreboding grew. 'Course we can.'

Dana watched with guarded eyes until he'd sat down on the sofa-end closest to her chair. She avoided making eye contact with him, sat down, then took a breath. 'I've been awake half the night thinking.'

He nodded, his voice soft. 'Me too.'

'This is a mess.' She laughed a small, nervous laugh. 'I mean, really, one hell of a mess.'

'It'll get better.'

She glanced at his face and away. 'Will it? Not if we don't lay some ground rules, it won't.'

Ground rules? He leaned forward, resting his elbows on his knees and linking his fingers together. He studied the top of her bowed head, keeping his voice low. 'Like what, exactly?'

'I don't want anyone else to know I'm pregnant.' She managed to look into his eyes for a split second. 'My family knows; your family knows. That's more than enough for now.'

Okay. That seemed fair enough. Time would tell the world anyway. He smiled slightly at the thought. Lord, but she was going to be something else as she filled out with baby. He wondered if she knew that.

'That's fine.'

'And you can't buy anything else for the baby.'

He frowned. 'Why not? You'll need things. I've been reading up, and there's a ton of stuff you'll need.'

She looked across at him in surprise. 'You've been reading up? Really?'

He cleared his throat and glanced away. 'Yeah, well. It seemed like the practical thing to do. You may have done this before. I haven't.'

Her blue eyes studied him intently for a moment. It seemed that every time she had him pegged, personality-wise, he would go and do something to recategorise himself again. Dana hated that about him. It knocked her off guard. Every damn time. And if there was one thing she'd learnt about Adam-flipping-Donovan it was that she shouldn't ever be off guard around him.

She smiled, much against her better judgement. 'That makes sense.'

He smiled back. 'I thought so.'

'And what did you learn?'

The smile grew broader. 'Mostly that you need to be asking for dry crackers around about now.'

Dana laughed.

The sound caught him by surprise and he stared at her with the same smile on his mouth. Her eyes sparkled with amusement. Aha, yet another of those Danas.

She looked away again, studying her feet for a moment as she brought her thoughts back to the reason she was there. But as she studied her feet her mind wandered to hoping that she wouldn't be able to see them in a few months.

With a small cough she cleared her throat. 'Promise me you won't buy any more stuff.'

He leaned forward slightly, his voice hoarse. 'Tell me why.'

She swallowed and glanced up at him, her cheeks warming. 'Because it's bad luck.'

One fair eyebrow disappeared beneath his unruly fringe, and then understanding entered his eyes. 'You don't want me to buy any stuff because if anything happens it'll be left as a reminder of what we lost.'

The words, spoken out loud, ripped at his chest in a way he'd never experienced before. He moved to stand up, to get closer to her so he could hold her. As if holding her to reassure her would have the same effect on him.

But Dana was quicker to move into an upright position, and was out of his reach faster than butter off a hot knife. She paced opposite him, using the long wooden chest in the centre of his room as a protective barrier of sorts.

'There's just all this stuff you don't understand, and I think you need to understand so that you don't keep—'

'Blundering in like an elephant at a tea party?'

She glanced at him from the corner of her eye. 'Something like that.'

'Okay. I'm listening.' He leaned back on the sofa again and folded his arms.

'You have to realise that there's really no need for you to get so involved in everything at this stage—'

'Everything like…?'

'Well.' She stopped for a second and waved her arm in front of her body. 'Everything. Like my life, my family, Jess—that kind of thing. There's really no point at this stage.'

He didn't like where her reasoning was leading. 'Go on.'

'It's just that there is really a very real chance that I won't carry full term.' She cleared her throat and started pacing again. Not looking at him was easier, so she talked to the floor, the walls, the windows—anywhere but to his face. 'And you need to accept that.'

His jaw clenched.

'And if that happens then you'll have spent all this time and effort involving yourself in the lives of people you'll have no need to see again.' She risked a glance in his direction. 'It's not like you were involved in their lives before.'

He stared her straight in the eye until she looked away, then rolled his neck to release some of the tension there. He could feel a headache beginning across the back of his head.

'It's just—' She paced again. 'You have to realise that if you become a part of some of those people's lives and then I lose this baby, when you leave some of those people may get hurt.'

He asked in a soft voice, his breath held still for a moment, 'Like who?'

She stopped and turned on him with wide eyes. 'Like Jess, for instance!' She placed a hand on her hip. 'Apparently she quite likes you.'

The breath came out. 'Though God alone knows why?'

She blinked. 'What?'

He took a breath and leaned forward again. 'You forgot to say "Though God alone knows why." It was what you were thinking, right?'

It wasn't. Well, it would have been fairly recently. But it wasn't any more. In fact the *All Things Good* list was getting longer the more time she spent with him. At some point during her long hours of thought she'd even had to admit to herself that it wouldn't just be Jess who would miss having him around if he wasn't there any more. And in that moment of realisation she'd known that this thing just couldn't keep going. What she was doing was damage control. Pure and simple.

Adam looked around his apartment for a moment as he thought, then stunned her with, 'Dana, do I remind you of Jim?'

She frowned. 'What? Where the hell did that come from?' She looked around where he'd looked, as if she'd find the answer sitting on a chair or a desk somewhere nearby. 'Why would you think that?'

He shrugged, placing his elbows back on his knees again. 'It seems to be the general consensus in your family, and you've got to admit we look a little alike.'

'No, you don't.'

He raised both eyebrows at her slightly raised voice. 'Really?'

'Well, except that you're both tall and fair-haired. There's no other resemblance.'

'None at all?' He didn't look as if he believed her, and he knew he didn't. 'So when you first met me it didn't occur to you that I was maybe like him in some way? And because you were hurting from him you took it out on me?'

Dana gasped, her mouth opening in surprise. 'Is that what you think?'

Adam studied her face, then took a deep breath and shrugged his shoulders. 'Hell, I don't know.'

She continued to stare at him, refusing to allow herself to deny any further something that might, just possibly, hold an element of truth in it. The simple matter was that he *did* look a little like Jim in height, build and colouring But the resemblance ended there. She knew that now.

But was it the reason she'd been so anti-Adam when she'd first met him? And since? It would make sense She'd met him while she'd still been smarting from all the mistakes that had been made, when everything had still been raw. And there he'd been. This devastatingly attractive man who, pre-Jim, would have been exactly the kind of man she'd have noticed from across a crowded room. Had she been fighting that attraction all along?

'Are you still in love with him?'

Her eyes grew wider, as much at her own realisation as at the question. Knowing that she might have been attracted to Adam from the start made her defensive mode kick in hard. 'What would it matter to you if I was? I wouldn't be your problem.'

Adam hated her answer the minute it left her lips. 'I guess it wouldn't. But apparently that doesn't stop me from asking.'

'Just so long as you don't expect an answer.' Dana continued to stare at him, her heart beating erratically. Oh yeah. *As if.* As if she was going to stand and tell him what she'd just started to realise herself. And as if she would confess to him what a failure her marriage had been. How she'd sought something from that relationship that didn't exist in exactly the same way her damned traitorous heart would like there to be something more in *this* relationship

Oh, no way. She was a realist now. Life had seen to that, hadn't it? She couldn't afford another mistake that big—for herself, her daughter, or the new life she hoped so dearly would make it into the world. That was why she was here now. To sort things. To be realistic.

Adam shook his head. She'd already answered him

hadn't she? Well, that didn't damn well mean he was going to accept what she was saying about other things.

'Whatever, Dana. But for the record—' He stood up and frowned hard when she took another step back from him. One long finger pointed straight at her and waggled up and down. 'I know exactly what you're doing with all this ground rules stuff, and I'm not playing.'

Dana watched as he moved away from the sofa and walked on silent feet across the open-plan room and into the kitchen area. 'Okay, what exactly am I doing?'

'You're trying the whole anally retentive control freak thing again. Carefully planning everything out, so it's all neat and organised.'

She followed him into the smaller area. 'It damn well needs *some* organising, don't you think?'

'Language, Dana.' He glanced over his shoulder as he opened a cupboard and lifted out a jar of coffee. He waggled the jar at her stomach. 'Our child can hear that.'

Dana spluttered angrily at his words and his oh-so-calm approach. 'You're a piece of work.'

'Maybe.' He moved towards the sink and filled the coffee pot. 'Maybe you just hate me right this second because you know I'm right.'

She stepped further into the small kitchen space, her eyes sparking with anger. 'Well, go on, then—if you're so very clever, you tell me how to make all this better.'

He turned so fast that she was caught off guard. Her eyes widened in surprise as he marched determinedly towards her, his eyes cold. Immediately she backed away, only to bang her back suddenly against the counter that separated the kitchen from the living room. One long, steel-like arm on either side of her imprisoned her against the cold surface.

Her mouth went dry.

Green eyes studied her up close for long, long moments. Though in actuality it was probably only a few seconds.

Dana's heart beat hard against her chest. She hadn't planned on this. After all those long hours of thinking she'd had it all set down to a 'T'. Hit and run. In with all the information, lay it all out, clearly and concisely, then leave. Get the hell out of town.

Adam obviously had different plans.

After what felt like a lifetime he spoke, his voice low. 'What did you think I'd do, Dana? Listen to this great plan of yours, nod and say goodbye? Until when?' He looked up as he thought, then back into her eyes. 'They wheel you into the delivery room?'

Her voice wobbled a touch as she answered, trying her very best to stay still so that her body wouldn't touch his. 'Maybe not quite that late. But something along those lines. You have to see it makes sense.'

'Do I?'

She nodded, her eyes dropping to his broad chest as she took short, sharp breaths. If she just took small breaths then she stood a fair chance of not brushing her breasts against that chest.

He stepped the tiniest bit closer, the movement drawing her eyes back to his. 'Shall I tell you what *I* think?'

She shrugged, a very small, carefully controlled *upward* movement that didn't bring her any closer to him. 'I get a choice?'

He pursed his lips as he mulled over the question, then smiled a barely perceptible smile. 'No.'

'Go on, then.'

'You're not getting rid of me. No matter what happens. I've told you that before and I meant it.' His voice was calm, matter-of-fact, and complete determination was written all over his face. 'No matter how much you try, or your family tries, I'm not going away. Because this baby—' he took his hands off the counter and placed them at her hips, so that his thumbs could brush over her rounded stomach at her belly button '—gives me the right to be here, no matter what anyone may think.'

Her bottom lip quivered and she closed her eyes to the exquisite bolt of pleasure his touch sent across her. This was exactly the kind of thing she'd been trying to avoid.

He continued moving his thumbs, as if the caress would hold their child safely in place. 'If you lose this baby it won't just be you losing it now. It'll be me too.'

He'd thought about it for half the night. Thought about the baby that was so determined to get into the world. Thought about how that baby would be *his* family, and thought about how much he was getting used to spending time with the family that was Dana and Jess. He already knew the rest of her family was great, and Jack was his best friend—or had been. It sort of all fitted—made perfect sense. The only thing that made it incomplete was the fact that Dana still loved her ex.

Blue eyes opened and blinked up at him.

He took a breath. 'If we lose this baby then I'm going to be right there, and we'll grieve together. And if not...' He smiled. 'Then I'll be in the delivery room for you to swear at and to ask for more painkillers.'

She felt her eyes fill up. Not again. She smiled and blinked hard at the same time. 'I always seem to end up crying around you. I hate that.'

He shrugged. 'It's hormonal.'

'You read that, did you?'

'I guess I must have.'

She sniffed, only too aware how unattractive it was.

Well, it was his own damned fault for making her cry. 'Is this the real you?'

He blinked slowly at the question. 'What do you mean?'

'This caring, thoughtful man who keeps appearing. Is that the real you, or are you the one I've been working with this last while?'

'The devastatingly attractive sex god who has women falling at his feet all day long?' His eyes sparkled with humour.

She rolled her eyes at the teasing tone of his voice. 'Oh, yeah, that'd be you right enough.'

'No.' He continued smiling as his voice lowered. 'I think you mean the sworn bachelor who would never allow himself to be tied down.'

A nod. 'That's the one I was thinking of. So which one are you?'

His head leaned a little closer as he whispered, 'I'm the tired one, who didn't sleep much last night and hasn't had coffee yet.'

Her eyes softened as she looked up at him. 'You're not a bad guy, you know. Your secret is out.'

'Just don't go telling everyone.'

'I'll try not to.'

'So, do you give in?' He raised an eyebrow in question and flashed her a smile complete with dimples.

In amongst her long night of thought, and the recent revelations brought into the open by their conversation, she admitted to herself she'd probably long since given in to him. Maybe even since before the fated reunion night. The minute she'd started making lists about him in her head was the minute she should have realised how much she had noticed him. And now that they had *that* night and the experience of this baby to hold them together she realised she was falling. Big-time. More every day.

It was the second biggest mistake of her life, unless she was very much mistaken.

As her thoughts wandered she raised her eyes to his fringe again. Her hand reached up to smooth it back and found itself caught halfway there by his. His fingers twined with hers.

'I'm not going away.'

She knew he meant the words. He would be there all the way through—would keep on doing this amazing protective thing he was so good at, and no doubt would make her fall all the harder for him the longer he stayed around. But he wouldn't love her. Not the way she needed him to.

She swallowed to loosen the lump in her throat, then leaned up and brushed her mouth across the corner of his. It was a truce of sorts. She would just have to deal with how she felt. It wasn't Adam's fault. He was just trying to do the right and decent thing. It was more than many men would have done in the same circumstances. It made her grateful that it was him.

'Thank you.'

He repeated the small kiss. 'You're welcome.'

Resisting the temptation to just stand in that one place and keep on kissing her, Adam stepped back and freed her from his hold. He'd won—this time. But the battles were getting more risky. There was a little more to lose each time, and the longer he involved himself with Dana and Jess the less he wanted to take a chance on being forced to let go.

But this time at least she wasn't going to push him back to arm's length and shut him out. He knew he couldn't have stood that. Couldn't have watched her from a distance, either grieving or growing large with his child, and not wanted to be there, right beside her, *involved*. Nope, he just couldn't have done that.

He might not have admitted during the long dark hours that there was any deeper meaning behind those feelings. But it had been a big step for him. One step at a time would have to do. He was standing dead centre in the middle of the notorious trap, and he didn't want to step out or escape. He wanted to see what came next.

Even if it meant spending more time getting attached to someone who was in love with someone else.

# CHAPTER TEN

'YOU okay?'

Dana blinked across at Tara. 'I feel like I'm being swept along on a huge wave and I can't get off, but apart from that I'm grand.'

Tara stood at the sink and looked out at Adam and Jess in the garden. Their laughter filtered through the open windows and she smiled. 'Jess gets on great with him, doesn't she?'

'Yes.' Dana sighed. 'She does.'

'Does he spend much time here now?'

'Oh, you know.' She moved her head from side to side as she sing-songed, 'Only every day.'

Tara looked over her shoulder with a raised eyebrow. *'Really?'*

Dana looked up at her from her design table and nodded. 'Yep.'

Yep, indeed. It was driving her crazy. Not so much the fact that he was in or around the house so much all of a sudden, but the fact that while there he was treating her like a pregnant sister or best buddy. She only had to bloody yawn and he had her tucked in with a duvet and a mug of warm milk. When warm milk was the very last thing she wanted to be tucked in with, thank you.

It was as if she wasn't even vaguely attractive any more. At least for a while there he'd still seemed to look at her in a kind of sexual manner. At one time she would have thanked the heavens for that small mercy. But Dana had undergone a fairly recent eye-opening when it came to Adam, and it now irritated her beyond belief. If she lacked sexuality to such an extent now, then she could only imagine how he would look at her when she was the size of a small house.

'I'm impressed.'

'Mmm.'

'Well, you have to admit...' Tara turned and leaned back against the deep sink. 'Who'd have thought it? Adam Donovan, family man.'

Dana glared at her wide grin. 'We're not a family.'

'Aren't you? That's what it looks like from the outside, honey.'

'Well, it's not what's happening.'

Tara watched as Dana tried to focus her attention on the design sketches laid out in front of her. She thought in silence for a few moments as the laughter continued to filter in from outside, then asked, 'So, whatever arrangement you two have will involve him being here every day after the baby is born too?'

'Am I going to have interrogation from every member of this family for the next few months on this?' She took a deep breath and looked up at Tara. 'Because I have to say it doesn't encourage me to call everyone for a wee chat.'

'They all care about you. It's what a family does.'

Her blue eyes swept towards the window. 'I'm holding up. If I need help I'll yell.'

'Will you?' Tara moved across the room and dragged a chair to sit facing Dana. She tilted her head to one side, her eyes full of questions. 'Because you do tend to do this highly organised, ''I'm in complete control of everything'' thing.'

Dana snorted slightly. 'Apparently not, or I wouldn't be in the position I'm in now, would I?'

'The pregnant position, or the in love with Adam position?'

Dana's eyes widened in surprise, darted to the open window and back again. Her voice dropped. 'What are you talking about?'

Tara smiled a small smile. 'I may write historical adventure stories to make ends meet, but I can recognise romance when I see it. This thing has been a ticking bomb ever since you went to work in that office.'

Dana opened her mouth to argue, thought for a second, and closed it again. Talking about it was more than overdue. It was just something she wasn't normally very good with. Her early days had trained her to stay quiet, to sort things on her own, not to trouble people. It was a hard thing to overcome. But could it really do any harm to try and make sense of the things that caused her to frown a little more every day? Well, no, it couldn't. So long as the conversation was *private*.

'Tara, this can't go out of this room...'

Tara waved a hand from side to side. 'Of course it can't. I haven't even told Jack what I think—and, believe me, that's taken an effort. I'm so used to talking to him about everything now that it's almost killed me. But he's spitting nails at the minute, so I thought it was best left be.'

Dana nodded. 'He hasn't spoken to Adam at all since last week. They need to sort it out, you know; it makes working together a tad strained.'

'Yeah, I know. If Jack shared an office with you two full-time, I think blood would have been shed by now.'

'It's sad.'

Tara sighed in agreement. 'It is. They're good friends.'

'I hope they can get past it.' She tapped her pencil

against the edge of her desk, pouting as she thought out loud. 'They're just both so bloody stubborn.'

Tara nodded, and they let a comfortable silence invade the distance between them as they both thought separate thoughts. Dana spoke first, her eyes curious. 'Did you know this might happen when you came up with the great makeover plot?'

'Not the pregnant bit, I didn't.'

Dana felt her cheeks warm. 'I didn't mean that.'

'The you and Adam getting together bit?' She watched as Dana nodded, noting how her blue eyes moved their focus to the window again. 'Yeah, it had occurred to me. What can I say? I guess I'm a romantic at heart. It happens when a person is happy, you see. You just want everyone else to feel the same way.'

When Dana looked back it was with a raised brow. 'And you thought two people who couldn't stand each other was the best plan?'

A shrug. 'I've seen the way you look at him sometimes. Those little…' she held her thumb and forefinger up, not quite touching, and peered at Dana with a squinting eye from behind the small gap created between them '…*minuscule* moments when you let your guard down.' She set her hand back down. 'I think you've quite *enjoyed* not liking him. I think it was safer for you.'

Dana stared and stared at her. Modern television chat shows had a lot to answer for, in her opinion. She placed a nonchalant look on her face and asked, 'And Adam?'

'Ah, Adam.'

'Yes, Adam.' She tilted her head forwards. 'You know—the man in the garden with my daughter. The father of my unborn child. The other ingredient in your little recipe for happiness. *That* Adam.'

'Sarcasm is another form of defensiveness, you know. Jack does it all the time—or did until he met me.'

Dana sighed. 'How can you even have thought he liked me when he was nothing but obnoxious the entire time? He did things and said things to deliberately annoy me every time he got a chance.'

'In response to the way you were around him, I'd guess.' Tara continued reasoning even as Dana's expression became more incredulous. 'No, I'm serious. You could wind him up without trying. And I think that's why I thought it might just work. Because I've never seen or heard of anyone getting to him that much. It had to mean something.'

'Yes, it did.' Dana nodded. 'That he didn't like me.'

'He liked you enough for you to be pregnant now.'

Dana leaned back against her chair and rubbed at her aching temples. It was all just too complicated. Nothing in her life could ever be simple, could it? Oh, no. She had long since reasoned that at some time in a previous life she must have been Jack the Ripper, or some equally evil person. Otherwise why did she keep having all this stuff happen to her every step of the way in this life? It was like some gigantic test. And Dana hated tests. Crosswords made her mad, for goodness' sake.

'C'mon, Dana, think about it.'

The headache was getting worse.

Tara continued, like a candidate pushing for re-election. 'He's always so calm and collected. In charge of everything he does. In every relationship he's ever been in he's been the one in control. Yet he only had to spend sixty seconds in a room with you and he was mad as hell.'

'It's called hatred.'

Tara grinned. 'Sweetheart, I think it's called frustration.'

Still rubbing at her head, Dana glanced across from between her fingers. 'Well, if I'm such a goddess then how come he's now treating me like I'm his bloody sister?'

'Ah.'

'Exactly. Ah.'

'No, I didn't mean "ah" as in, "Ah, my theory is wrong." I meant "ah" as in, "Ah, and who's frustrated now?"'

Dana lifted her hand away to glare dangerously.

'You are, aren't you?' The grin reappeared. 'Well, you don't need to tell me. Jack couldn't lay a finger on me for the first six weeks after we found out. It was cute for the first two, but after that...' She leaned forward to whisper, 'We're fine now,' and winked.

'*Oooh*, brother and sex conversation.' Dana pulled a face. 'Not happening, please.'

'You should try seducing him.'

'I should try what?'

'Seducing him.' Tara leaned back again. 'I'll bet money you could. Guys love it when their woman is pregnant. I think they actually find it sexy in a whole "I put that there" way. It boosts their ego.'

Dana blinked at her until she could eventually find words. 'You know you've been spending too much time around your friend Laura?'

Tara laughed musically at the reference to her outspoken friend. Nothing was sacred when it came to Laura. She had a very individual way of looking at the world. 'You know Jack sent Adam on a date with her once?'

'No, I didn't.' Jealousy gripped Dana like a bad cramp. 'When was that?'

'Oh, way back before we got married. Let's just say they didn't hit it off.'

'Gee, and you didn't immediately think it was a match made in heaven?'

'Come on, Dana.' Tara leaned forward and patted her arm. 'It can't be that bad. He's still here.'

Yes, he was. No doubt about that. Still there. But in body only. Not heart and soul. She sighed, the sadness sneaking through her defensive outer shell. 'For the baby, Tara. Not for me.'

'I think you're wrong about that.'

She shook her head. 'No. He'd have said something if there was more to it than that.' A weak smile appeared. 'He's not afraid to speak out, in case you hadn't noticed.'

'Maybe he doesn't think you feel the same way.'

'Are you saying you think he might be *nervous*?'

A shrug. 'Or scared of making a fool of himself. A lot of men are, you know.'

'Not this one.'

'Have you told him how *you* feel?'

'Hell, no.' Dana laughed. 'I'm not about to add my name to a long list.'

'You're each as bad as the other.' Tara shook her head and stood up, pushing her chair back into place. 'Well, one of you is going to have to take a chance at some point.' She leaned down to kiss her favourite sister-in-law on the cheek. 'It would be such a shame to miss it.'

Dana blinked into space long after Tara had gone. Then she shook her head. Nah. Adam Donovan didn't love her. Not the guy who considered himself the last bachelor on the planet.

He didn't know what the hell he wanted.

Adam wanted Dana.

It had sneaked up on him so suddenly that he hadn't

realised it until his second week of leaving Dana to come back to his empty apartment.

His mind had told him that there had to be a reason why he wanted a family life *now* but had never felt the need for it before. And the answer had come the night he had looked in on Dana reading with Jess in bed. She'd been sitting close to her daughter, her hair loose around her shoulders and her skin glowing in the soft light. He'd winked at Jess from the open doorway, and then Dana had looked up for a brief moment and smiled at him. And he'd just known.

He didn't know what he'd expected it to feel like. He'd always vaguely assumed it would be some great wave that would hit him, or some overwhelming passionate need that would point the direction. Instead it had taken one small, simple smile and he'd just known he was in love. No fanfares, no big crash. Just a warm certainty that this was where he should be. He'd never before felt such certainty. Such a sense of *belonging*.

But had he walked on in and told her? Had he waited 'til she left the room and swept her up into his arms? Whisked her off to the heaven he remembered from when they'd made the baby?

Had he hell.

He'd stood in the doorway with a lump the size of a fist in his throat and smiled back at her. And, big, brave guy that he was, he'd then turned and frowned his way down the hallway.

The picture would have been vaguely more right for a happy ending if the source of his new-found affection wasn't bloody well in love with someone else!

Punching his pillow, he rolled over to look into the darkness of his bedroom. He needed a plan. After all, he was Adam Donovan. He was a pretty damned terrific guy.

Women had been trying to tie him down for years, so he couldn't be all that bad. He thought about making a pros and cons list for himself. His mother had always done that kind of stuff—said it helped her make a decision. But it was—well, a girls' thing, wasn't it?

He just needed a plan.

He needed to find a way to make Dana look at him differently. She had to see he was responsible, that he'd be there. And not just because of the baby either.

A smile touched his mouth in the darkness. He wanted dozens of babies with her. He wondered how enthusiastic she'd be about that plan. But, hell, their kids would be great. Full of spirit and sheer bloody-mindedness. His seat-of-the-pants attitude towards life would balance out her deep-rooted need to be anally retentive. A match made in heaven.

All he had to do was convince Dana.

He'd have to show her he could take care of her, that they made a good team in *and* out of the office. Because even though they argued they'd always managed to wow the customers and make the sales. Their different person-alities added up to a winning combination. And, since they'd started talking, the atmosphere had definitely im-proved. All it had taken was a little work.

He was going to have to persuade her family that he was here to stay, whether they liked it or not. Persuade them that he was a better guy than Jim. Right now he knew they probably all thought he was dirt, and he had to admit that that—well, bruised him. He wanted them to like him—to approve of him, almost. He'd never sought approval from outsiders before. It was yet another new experience for him. This whole love thing really did change a person's perspective, he reflected with a rueful smile in the darkness.

His mind kept on turning. He was going to have to be there every day so Dana spent less time with her damn ex. After all, the guy had someone else now, didn't he? That meant *he'd* moved on. He just had to persuade Dana it was time she did the same. In his general direction, of course.

It just ate him up that Dana could still hold a candle for Jim when he, Adam, was such a great guy.

He'd have to convince her he wasn't a bachelor type after all. Convince her he could be a family man, a husband as well as a father. Even though he still worried on a daily basis about the fatherhood part. It would mean that she'd have to see he could treat her with respect and not try to jump on her at every available moment. Even if he *really* wanted to.

He could do all that. One step at a time.

Dana knew he was having some kind of a breakdown the minute she looked down the garden path.

'Where is your car?'

Adam just blinked at her. She hated it when he did that. 'Huh?'

'Your car.' She pointed down the driveway to the silver MPV that sat there. 'Where is it?'

He placed a hand to the small of her back and guided her along the path. 'That *is* my car.'

She stopped dead at the gate and turned to frown up at him. 'You changed your car for *that* thing?' She pointed at it again.

Adam looked at her as if she was being abnormal. 'Yes. What's the big deal? I was due a trade-in. I just traded for something a bit more practical. I don't see what's so strange about that.'

From beneath the frown her eyes searched his for some

sign that he was kidding her. A sparkle. A hint of a sparkle. Nope.

'Since when do you even look remotely in the direction of the word *practical*?'

Adam shrugged and lifted the latch on her gate before guiding her through it with a gentle push of his hand. 'It's my age.'

'You'd better not have bought this for the baby.'

He raised an eyebrow at her. 'The baby will be able to drive when it gets here?' He grinned. 'I guess any child of mine is going to be talented, but c'mon!'

Her mouth twitched. 'I mean it.'

'I bought it for me to drive.' He opened the door for her and reached across to buckle her seat-belt when she was in. He smiled then, his face close to hers. 'But you have to admit it was going to be tough to fit a baby chair into a sports car.'

Dana was momentarily distracted by how close he was as he spoke the soft words. He smelled good. God, he smelled *great*, and he looked so delicious close up. She swallowed to moisten her dry throat. 'Possibly.'

His smile upgraded to a grin. 'You hate it when I'm right.'

'Yes, I do.' She watched his every move as he closed her door and sprinted round to pull open the driver's door. 'But I still think it breaks the ''no buying anything for the baby'' rule.'

Still grinning at her as he fastened his own seat-belt, he winked. 'Babes, this thing has a turbo engine and real nice alloys, a leather interior, and anything that can be electrical *is* electrical.' He ran one large hand over the steering wheel. 'There's still testosterone in this vehicle, don't you worry.'

Dana laughed.

His green eyes sparkled as he turned his head to reverse the car back. 'You should do that more often.'

'Laugh at the fact that you're an idiot?'

'Laugh in general.'

'Are you suggesting I don't ever laugh?'

'No.' He continued to shine his dimples at her. 'I just think you don't do it often enough. Someone told me once that happy mother equals happy baby.'

Everything for the baby, right? She glanced away from him to hide her eyes. 'I'm happy enough, Adam. I'll be happier when the doctor says we're doing okay.'

A hand reached off the gearstick to squeeze one of the ice-cold hands in her lap. 'She will, babe. I guarantee it.'

'You're just so all-fired sure of yourself, aren't you?'

He nodded as he kept looking through the windscreen. 'Yep.'

'In absolutely everything?'

'Uh-huh.'

'Nothing ever fazes you?'

'Nope.' He managed the lie without losing a beat. He was sitting beside the one thing that had fazed him more than anything else ever had in his life. But she didn't need to know that just yet.

Dana took a deep, silent breath as she studied his profile. *Mmm.* And Tara honestly thought this guy was in love with her? Dana shook her head. He was so damned sure of everything he did that if he loved her she'd already be halfway up the aisle.

'I can't see it.'

Dana smiled in his direction. 'It's right there on the screen.'

Adam leaned in closer to the flickering screen and stared. 'Nope. This is obviously one of those things your eyes need to be trained for.' When he glanced at her he frowned, a look of regret showing through on his face. 'I suppose this makes me a crap father?'

He was concerned? She recognised the emotion in his eyes. Recognised it, but was surprised to see it there.

Sitting upright, she took his large hand in hers. 'Don't be dumb. It doesn't make you a crap father. Here—' She straightened out his forefinger and led it to the screen, tracing the shape of their baby for him. 'That's the head, the body, that's the legs, and that's an arm.'

He stared in fascination, then looked at the serene smile that reached from her mouth to her eyes. Slowly he brought her hand to his mouth and kissed her palm, smiling at her as he lowered it again. 'Thank you.'

Dana's heart flip-flopped painfully inside her chest. If she hadn't already known she was falling in love with him she would sure as hell have known now. She swallowed hard, her voice coming out a little on the crackly side. 'A lot of people don't see it first time.'

'I meant for the baby.'

Her heart did it again. Much more of this and he was going to have to take her down the hallway to the cardiology unit.

Adam kept hold of her hand as he spoke. 'You didn't have to go through with this, but you did. I just thought you should know I'm glad.'

She blinked. 'You are?'

'Yes, I am.'

She allowed a doubt to surface. 'You're not doing all this out of a sense of duty, are you, Adam? Because I'd understand completely if you couldn't keep all this care and attention going. You could just go to the check-ups and see me in work until after the birth, and then we could arrange something else.'

He frowned. 'Is that what you want me to do?'

She glanced away. 'It's entirely your decision.'

'You're saying my being around isn't helping any?'

She wouldn't lie about that. 'No, I'm not saying that.'

'Am I cramping your style?'

Her eyes glanced up again. 'What?'

'Maybe my being there is affecting the number of time Jim comes over.'

Dana's eyebrow rose at the statement. Why in God' name would his being there affect Jim coming to see Jess 'I appreciate your concern, Adam, but, really, your being there doesn't stop Jim from coming over. He's been away that's all. He'll be around for Jess's birthday.'

Adam nodded, studying their two joined hands. 'Great.'

*Great?* He thought that was great? What was he now' A personal friend of Jim's?

As he glanced upwards and smiled she could still see the concern in his eyes. It couldn't do so much harm to give just a little, could it? 'I am glad you're around.'

'You are?' His eyes sparkled at her.

She pulled her hand away. 'Oh, and you needn't bother your ass getting all smug about that either. You're useful.' She folded her arms across her chest and looked sideways at him. 'Occasionally. And Jess really does like you. I'm just saying if you want to skip a day or two to make way for the rest of your life, then that's fine.'

Adam's smile grew. She was glad he was around. That was a plus. And the fact that she was now being argumentative about it meant it was true. Score one to him. And the car had worked too.

The plan was going well. Next up was the 'better than Jim' stage.

# CHAPTER ELEVEN

ADAM was up to something. Dana just knew it. It was his damned cheerful whistling. It gave him away and it was making her crazy!

Okay, so maybe crazier was a better description.

She could only actually blame pregnancy hormones for so much. The crying, weepy female thing, which was just so not her: that had to be hormones. Though it had to be said being in love with someone who wasn't in love with her probably didn't help much.

But as for the sexual frustration…

Not only would it not go away, Dana was fairly sure she couldn't blame it on her hormones. Well, not because she was pregnant anyway. Surely it followed that if she was already with child her hormones shouldn't still be crying out for the completion she'd experienced in that one unforgettable night? So what could the explanation be?

The only reasonable explanation was the simple fact that she wanted Adam. Was, since fairly recently, obsessed with Adam.

It made her hate him. But at least that was familiar ground.

After the fourth day of whistling she snapped. 'Okay, do you want to tell me what the hell's going on?'

Adam stopped whistling and glanced across at her. He folded over their application for space at a Perfect Homes exhibition they were joining in Dublin and placed it inside a heavy envelope.

'Well, I've finished the application, and now I've put it in an envelope.' He held it up and reached for another small piece of paper which he waved as he smiled at her. 'With its friend, Mr Cheque.'

Dana watched with narrowed eyes as Mr Cheque went into the envelope and Adam's tongue ran along the seal. She reminded herself to breathe out. This was getting truly ridiculous. Now the man couldn't even lick a damned envelope without her noticing!

'I wasn't talking about the application.'

Adam blinked. 'You weren't?'

He knew rightly she wasn't, and she knew from the gleam in his eye that he knew. She took a deep breath and tried to remain calm. 'No, I wasn't. I'm referring to the whistling.'

'The whistling.' He nodded wisely and leaned back in his chair, moving it from side to side as he studied her. 'Of course.'

'You've been doing it for days now.'

'Have I?'

Another deep, calming breath. 'Yes, you have. And I want to know what's going on.'

'Whistling, apparently.'

'You're up to something.' She waggled a swatch of material at him. 'And I know it.'

'Well, if you know it, you can tell me what it is then— can't you?'

Her blue eyes studied his smiling face intently. She gritted her teeth as she did it. He was making her insane.

Deep breath, deep breath, and count to twenty. Twenty because ten didn't quite do the trick. She managed a fake smile. 'If I knew I wouldn't need to ask you.'

He glanced down, took a moment to control his smile, and glanced up at her from beneath thick fair hair. 'You really are very distrustful of me, even after all this time, aren't you?'

'Because you're damn well up to something, Adam!'

She leaned back after the angry words had left her mouth. With a frown she glared across at his smiling face. She hated that he was always so in control of everything—while everything was just getting further and further out of *her* control with every day.

'Maybe it's a surprise.'

His softly spoken words stunned her into momentary silence, then she somehow managed to answer. 'A surprise for me?'

'In a roundabout way.'

'I hate surprises.'

With a flash of a grin he went back to addressing his envelope. 'Only because you don't get to control them.'

His jibe was so close to the mark that she wanted to kill him. What was he now? A mind-reader? Madame Adam?

'I hate you.'

'No, you don't.'

She laughed sarcastically as she shuffled the swatches of material in front of her. 'Oh, right this second I do.'

Adam stood and walked across to sit on the edge of her desk, smiling down at her as he pointed to a dark russet. 'That one. And, no, you don't. Deep down you know that we keep each other on our toes, that's why we're never bored.'

She pushed away the swatch he had indicated, despite the fact that up until the moment he'd touched it it had been her own first choice. 'So this surprise of yours is to keep me on my toes, is it? What's wrong? You afraid there's not enough going on in my life at the minute to keep me occupied?'

He watched as she pushed forward a deep gold, shaking his head and reaching for the russet again. 'Would you prefer it if I was some dull bank manager type whose every move could be predicted a week in advance?'

There had been a time in her life when she would have preferred exactly that. But now...

Now she *did* like his unpredictability, even found it vaguely stimulating. But only when she could figure out what he was doing before he made it obvious or explained it to her. It meant she was, in some way, smart enough to keep up with him. Still in control, she guessed. Safe.

Ha! Safe had long since passed. Now, in order to survive, she needed to know how his mind worked—needed to know he wasn't about to pull some stunt that would have her crying all over the place again—or worse still losing it and telling him she was in love with him. Because every time he did something thoughtful or considerate or vaguely in the region of caring she would smile at him and the words would jump up into her mouth. She had to purse her lips to stop them before they escaped. And that meant being forearmed was an absolute imperative.

'I would prefer it if you didn't go about doing the whole smug whistling thing, and I would prefer it if you would consult with me about any surprises.'

Adam's mouth twitched. He lifted the russet swatch and studied it intently before looking up at her with a steady green gaze. 'I'll take all that into consideration.'

'Because what I think matters to you?'

He ignored the sarcasm in her voice and leaned forward to lay the swatch across her shoulder. 'Yes, it does.'

She watched hypnotised as he ran his knuckles along the swatch, before catching her hair between his thumb and forefinger and smoothing it past her shoulder and along the edge of her breast. Her breath caught. There went her precious control again.

His voice dropped to a seductive whisper. 'But I'm still not telling you what it is.'

She watched in shock as he grinned, got up off the desk and snatched up his envelope. He grabbed his coat from the rack by the door and glanced over his shoulder.

'That colour—and we both know it. Maybe one day you might just stop arguing with me.' He winked. 'After all, we both know how successful a team we are when we don't argue.'

The office door closed and whistling sounded through from the reception area. Dana sat and stared at the door for an eternity, his words echoing in her ears. *We both know how successful a team we are when we don't argue.* What the holy hell did he mean by that? She mulled the words over. He couldn't possibly mean... Her eyes widened.

Then she shook her head. That man was up to something.

Adam was nervous.

No. He scratched that thought. Nervous didn't cover it. He raised his chin an inch or two after his car was parked and looked out of the window at the other cars already there. He was a man. He could do this. He could face a place full of people who probably wanted him dead and his body parts shipped to different time zones.

There was a noise from the back of his car and he smiled. The surprise was getting restless.

'Why is Adam here?'

Dana blinked at her brother's tone. 'Because he was invited.'

'This is a family thing.'

She shook her head. 'No, this is Jess's birthday, and she invited him. And anyway...' She waited until Jack's eyes met hers. 'You can't go on hating him for ever. He's your friend, for crying out loud, and technically he is now a member of the family—in a roundabout way.'

Jack seemed to consider her words carefully before answering. 'Are you two in a relationship of some kind now?'

'Sort of. But not in the way you think.'

'Would you like to be?'

She turned her eyes back to the assortment of food she was laying out on the long trestle table, avoiding his direct gaze. 'That's not really any of your business. But I'll tell you one thing, Jack.' She looked back at him. 'You can think of him as the evil guy who got your innocent sister pregnant on a one-night stand all you want, but it takes two to tango.'

'Are you telling me you wanted to get pregnant?'

'No.' She sighed. 'I'm not telling you that. But I'm saying it wasn't done against my will either. What happened between us was a mutual, caught-up-in-the-moment kind of thing. I'm as much to blame as Adam is. So there's no point in you laying all the blame at his door.'

Jack opened his mouth, thought for a moment, then closed it again. He took a breath. 'It's not like you to stick up for him. I thought you thought he was slime.'

'Obviously not, Jack, or I wouldn't be pregnant right now.' She pointed out what had been pointed out to her so many times of late. 'And I've got to know him better now. He has his good points.'

She looked up and smiled at Jack's look of suspicion. One hand reached out to rub his arm. 'If he was slime he wouldn't have stood by me through this. He didn't even have to see this child if he didn't want to, never mind be there for me too.' She risked a squeeze before removing her hand. 'Adam is a decent man deep down.'

Jack reached his long arms forward and pulled his sister into a hug. 'I know that. Knew that before you did, actually, sis.'

'You've just chosen to forget recently.' She looked up at him from his wool-covered chest. 'He misses you.'

Jack grinned down. 'Did he tell you that?'

'Hell, no.' She grinned back. 'But if he got to spend more time with you again he wouldn't be here making me crazy every day.'

'Now you're looking to get rid of him?'

She hid her face. 'The odd day, maybe.'

Jack continued to hold her in the haven of his hug. He might be the youngest of them all, but he'd always tried to look out for his sisters. 'You really care about him.'

Dana knew it was a statement of fact rather than a question. She nodded against his chest.

Jack nodded too. He'd figured as much.

He took a deep breath that pushed Dana's head out and back. 'Well, just for the record, I am still going to have to hit him.'

Dana looked up at his familiar face. 'Why?'

'It's a guy thing.' He shrugged. 'I'm old-fashioned.'

She simply stared.

Jack smiled. 'But as he's a friend, and I care about you both, I promise I'll only swing the once.'

'That's probably all he'll let you do.'

Jess loved her surprise. She squealed with delight as Adam handed the end of the lead to her. 'This is for me? Really, really for me?'

Adam's face lit up. 'Yes, really, really for you. Happy birthday.'

Jess's small arms encircled the Labrador's neck. 'I love her!'

'Him.'

She stood and threw her arms around Adam's waist. 'And I love you. You're the best.'

Adam felt his throat grow tight as he hunched down to hug Dana's daughter to him. He'd wanted to show everyone he was a great guy by putting so much thought into his gift, but he hadn't realised how much Jess's simple, honest words would mean. She was an amazing kid—so like her mother that it made him smile. Knowing how much he loved the adult version, he should have realised how much he'd grown to care for the junior version too.

The dog jumped up and licked at their ears, which sent Jess into a fit of the giggles. 'What's his name?'

'BJ. And don't look at me—the name was already there.'

'I like it.'

'Me too.'

He watched as she ran back up the pathway, the large black dog bounding along at her side. With a deep breath he followed her into the assembled crowd of adults, noting the heads that turned his way and the whispers along the edges.

Tara walked out of the crowd and linked her arm with his. 'Hey, there.'

He smiled down at her, leaning his head to speak in a low voice. 'What are you, then? The cavalry?'

Tara grinned. 'Something like that. Great present, by the way.'

'I liked it.'

'So does Jess.' She stopped alongside Lauren and Rachel. 'Adam, you've met Dana's sisters before, haven't you?'

Both women smiled politely at him. Lauren, with a sparkle in her eyes, was the first to break the ice. 'We've met a time or two. But that was before you became a father, I believe.'

His eyes widened in shock at her words, then a low rumble of laughter left his chest. 'That's true. It's good to see you, Lauren. Michael here?'

Lauren glanced around the garden for a glimpse of her husband. 'Mmm, he's currently fishing Rachel's two-year-old out of the flowerbeds. He's going through a fascination with dirt.'

'We don't actually grow out of that.'

She nodded. 'Oh, I know.' Her eyes, a shade or two paler than Dana's, looked back up at him. 'You've done quite a bit round this place, Adam. It looks great.'

Rachel nodded in agreement. 'Everyone has commented on it. I don't know how you managed to get Dana to agree to let you do all that stuff. She'd have bitten off our heads before she'd have let us help.'

'Or volunteer our husbands to help.'

Adam smiled. That certainly sounded like the Dana he knew. 'She can be a tad independent-minded.'

'She can be one stubborn—'

He laughed and interrupted Rachel. 'Yeah, that too.'

Lauren, who was rapidly taking on the role of outspoken member of the family, waded on in. 'We hear you've been spending a lot of time here.'

Adam raised an eyebrow as he looked down at Tara.

Tara shrugged elegantly. 'News travels fast in this family.'

Lauren continued. 'So, you planning on getting married?'

Adam felt a flush touch his neck. This was actually worse than he had imagined. His eyes searched for Dana as he answered. 'We haven't discussed it.'

'Meaning you're going to discuss it?'

He located her near the back of the house, where Jess was showing her the surprise. Adam noted that Dana didn't exactly look pleased.

'We might get round to it.'

'Because you think you should, or because you want to?'

He glanced back with a small smile as his flush moved in a northerly direction. 'Have you ever considered working for the police?'

Lauren raised an eyebrow in an all too familiar manner. 'Michael has asked me that a time or two.'

'You should. You'd be good.' He looked back again as Dana moved, and saw that Jim stood beside her. He frowned.

'Honey, if you think *I've* got a load of questions then you need to avoid Tess for the rest of the afternoon. She has a million of them for you, and I'll swear she carries a spotlight with her specifically for those question sessions. As kids we were all scared stiff when we were given a secret to keep.'

Rachel continued. 'She could get blood from a stone. And she's looking to talk to you in a bad way.'

Adam felt his chest tighten as Jim said something and Dana reached out to turn him back towards the house. She spoke over her shoulder to Jess, who in turn hung her head slightly and turned to pull BJ back towards the garden. But the moment the dog bounded forward her face was transformed back to a smile again.

Tara tugged on his arm. 'You okay?'

He smiled down at her. 'Yeah, fine. Avoid Tess, the scary eldest sister. Gotcha.'

He managed to make it inside to Dana after another exhausting twenty minutes of questioning. His mind was working non-stop as to what Dana and her ex could have got up to in that time. Jealousy was an ugly thing.

When he found her she was alone.

'Hey.'

She glared across at him from the sink. 'I was wondering how long it would take for you to pluck up the courage to come see me.'

He shrugged and leaned against the door-frame, filling the small doorway. 'Your family wouldn't let me away—what can I say? I'm their favourite topic of conversation at the minute.'

'Oh, I know.'

He watched as she ripped a lettuce with more vengeance than necessary. 'What did that poor vegetable do to you?'

'It didn't bring my daughter a dog without discussing it with me. That's for certain!'

'You're ticked off about the dog?'

'Not as much as Jim is.' She turned to frown at him, leaning her hip against the sink. 'You shouldn't have done it, Adam. Not today. You outshone her father on her birthday.'

He frowned at her words. 'I wasn't trying to turn it into a competition. I thought Jess would like it.'

'Really? And it didn't enter your head that your present would be better than his?'

He'd been trying to show he was better than Jim for Dana, but for Jess he'd actually just wanted to show everyone that he could be thoughtful in what he did. A great guy, in fact. Annoying Jim was certainly a bonus, though. 'What did he get her?'

Dana's face flushed. 'That's not the point.'

'No, come on—what did he get her that I managed to outshine with some mangy stray?'

There was a tense silence as Dana's chest heaved, and Adam raised an eyebrow in question. 'He gave her money.'

'He gave her money?' Adam's eyes widened in disbelief. 'He gave his own daughter money in a card? Hell, Dana, I could have bought her a bag of sweets and I'd have made more of an effort!'

'But you didn't. You bought her a dog. A friend for life. How is he supposed to look like a great father when competing against that kind of thoughtfulness?' Her eyes glistened.

Adam stepped into the room, his anger growing. How in hell could she keep sticking up for this guy? Was she completely blind when it came to him?

'He could try being more thoughtful—maybe talking to her and finding out what she'd like! It's what I did. She's wanted a dog for for ever, from what she's said.'

'Well, he's not like you.'

'You're damn right he's not.' He stopped right in front of her and glared down at her flushed face. 'And the sooner you realise that the better.'

She opened her mouth to protest, only to be silenced when he cupped her face with his large hands and pushed his mouth to hers. She was mad at him, so she attempted a struggle, but it was a feeble attempt. After all, she'd been fairly desperate to be kissed again by him for an age now. After a moment she stepped into his body and grabbed the front of his shirt with her small hands. At *last*.

The kiss changed from punishment to something softer the minute she moved in and moulded her body against his. With a groan he moved his hands to wrap her waist in his arms. *At last.* It had taken all his control to keep his hands off her this last while. Now he decided that if she couldn't see he was more of a man than her ex then he was just damned well going to have to show her. At every available opportunity, if that was what it took.

Eventually he raised his head to look down at her.

Dana lifted her heavy eyelids and blinked at him. At last she managed to speak. 'You kissing me doesn't make what you did right.'

He released her and stepped away, his jaw clenched. 'What exactly do you want me to do? Apologise to him?'

'Maybe you should. You took something away from him today.'

'And that still matters to you?' He frowned down at her as he asked the question.

Dana studied his face, then nodded as she looked down. 'I can't help it, Adam. He's her father. He's supposed to be the one to put the smile on her face that you just did. I can't let anyone take that away from her, or him. And today you did.'

The punch knocked him to one side.

'I owed you that one.'

With the back of one hand pressed against his bleeding lip, he glanced at Jack from the corner of his eye. 'I just can't get away from the Lewis family today, can I?'

Jack stepped forward and watched as Adam squared his shoulders in preparation. 'Hey, ease up there, champ. I'm only swinging the once. I owed you that for going behind my back.'

Jack had, and Adam had been expecting it. He'd actually hoped it would come sooner rather than later, for the sake of their friendship.

Having left Dana in a cloud of anger, he'd taken a walk to the stream in the wilderness at the end of her long garden. He wasn't leaving—or quitting, for that matter. Oh, no, he just needed a minute or two to regroup and get round the fact that she was still so damned in love with Jim.

He just hadn't expected to be thumped when he eventually got five seconds' peace.

'So that's it, then?' He eyed Jack with suspicion.

'Yep. Unless you've done anything else I should be hitting you for?' An eyebrow raised in question.

'Not unless you're mad about the dog too.'

'The dog?'

'Never mind.' With a resigned nod he sat down on a long wooden bench facing the water. 'Okay, just so long as you're only swinging the once. I guess I deserved that much.'

'Yes, you did. You should have told me. I shouldn't have had to find out the way I did. You see, I was under the impression that you and I were mates.'

'We were.' Adam shook his head as he fumbled in a pocket for a handkerchief to hold against his lip. 'We are. And you're right. I should have told you. I would have. Everything just got real complicated. It still is. I just don't have much control over my life any more. I'm sorry.'

Jack studied his profile before nodding, grunting, 'Okay, then,' and sitting down beside him. They both leaned forward, forearms on knees, and watched the water flow on by. Eventually Jack spoke up again. 'Did you two have another row?'

'Something like that.'

'About the dog, I'm guessing?'

Adam nodded. 'Apparently I've made Jim look like a bad father by getting Jess exactly what she wanted instead of money in an envelope. I can't win.'

Jack sighed. 'He doesn't need any help looking like a bad father. He can do that all on his own.'

'Dana doesn't seem to think so.'

'Dana does her best to try and make him into a good father for Jess. That's all.' He smiled at the water. 'You know Jim's allergic to dogs?'

Adam's mouth twitched and he grimaced at the pain. He held his hand up to his split lip again, glancing sideways at Jack. 'Jess may have mentioned it.'

Jack grinned. 'That's my boy.'

They both turned their attention back to the water. Jack gave Adam a moment or two longer to think. 'So, you're moping down here because my sister gave out to you about the dog?'

'I'm not moping.'

'No?'

'No.' He frowned in a sideways glance. 'I'm regrouping.'

'You make dealing with Dana sound like a military campaign.'

'Probably because most of the time it is.'

Jack studied him for a moment, then asked the big question. 'You figure out why it matters yet?'

Adam took a deep breath. 'Yep. Got that one.'

Jack's grin reappeared. 'Takes a little time sometimes. I remember that much.'

Adam laughed. 'At least Tara wasn't still in love with an ex-husband. You had it easy.'

Jack's eyes widened. 'You think Dana is still in love with Jim?'

'Yes.' He turned his head to add sarcastically, 'Unless you feel like telling me she's not.'

Jack shrugged. 'She's not.'

'Then why is she so mad about the damn dog?'

Jack studied his friend's look of confusion, the challenge in his eyes to prove him wrong. As with any man, it would take Jack some quick talking to convince Adam he had actually got it wrong. He quite obviously believed he'd got it completely right.

'Probably because it's so easy for you to keep pointing out his failings to Jess, and Dana tries so hard to protect her from all that. She doesn't want her daughter to realise what a complete moron he can be.' Jack smiled as he continued, 'You see, you're a thinker. You see what people need and try your best to find a way to give it to them. It's part of the reason you make such a great business partner. Guess it was only a matter of time before it spilled over into your personal life.'

Adam shrugged off the compliment. 'If he's such a moron then why did she marry him?'

Jack took a deep breath. 'Ours is a long and complicated family history. I always thought it was because she just wanted so badly to be married—to make the perfect family that we hadn't had growing up. Jim just happened to be the first one to ask. But maybe her reasons were different. Have you tried asking her?'

Adam frowned. 'No.'

'Or telling her now how you feel?'

He looked away. 'I'm getting round to it. I have a plan.'

Jack studied his profile again. 'Oh, well, if you have a *plan*.'

Adam let his eyes focus on the water again as he thought. He smiled slightly as he realised he'd been doing the one thing that he'd been so critical of Dana for.

Keeping control of everything. Planning it all meticulously and trying to keep ahead of the game. Life just wasn't like that, he realised. Sometimes a person just had to go out there and say what he wanted. Take a chance.

'Being a bachelor was a lot simpler than this, you know.'

'Hell, I know.' Jack grinned as Adam turned towards him. 'But I tell you, being a husband and father has more than enough of its own rewards too.'

# CHAPTER TWELVE

WHY couldn't she just have met Adam before she'd met Jim?

The question had been in her mind even before he walked into the kitchen, twenty minutes after Adam had left it. If she could just have met someone who was as genuinely warm-hearted, as Adam had in the end turned out so obviously to be. Warm-hearted but with an edge of genuine potent testosterone in him that kept her blood humming in her veins. A man with that combination could have kept her blissfully happy for the rest of her days.

But she'd met Jim Taylor instead. Met him and married him. Because she'd thought that would be her happily ever after—her chance to make right all the things her mother had got wrong. She was going to be the best wife, the best mother, make sure everything would be perfect.

When the marriage had started to go wrong she'd tried hard to fix it, to make things work out. They hadn't. And since they hadn't, she'd tried every year at Jess's birthday and at Christmas to make him seem like the kind of father her daughter deserved. So that her daughter wouldn't suffer from the mistake her mother had made. So that Dana herself wouldn't fail in pretty much the same way her own mother had done. She'd failed this time because of a dog. And every year it was getting a little harder—because every year her daughter was becoming more aware. It was like trying to keep Santa Claus alive for those few extra years. Conserving the magic somehow.

Adam, meanwhile, whether he realised it or not, was

going to make one hell of a father. Dana believed that as surely as she believed the sun would rise each morning.

She watched as Jess and her numerous cousins threw a stick for BJ who dutifully ran to fetch it and brought it back. A huge sloppy grin was permanently plastered all over the dog's face and it made Dana smile. She'd almost lay odds that Adam had picked him because of that grin. He'd have understood it, somehow.

'It'll have to go.'

Dana took a calming breath.

'The dog or your daughter?'

'You know exactly what I mean.'

'Yes, I do.' She ran a hand across her poor aching forehead. 'And it's not going anywhere. You only have to look at Jess's face to see how much she loves that dog. I should have got her one years ago.'

Jim moved a step forward, bringing himself directly into her line of vision as she turned from the window. 'You know I'm allergic, so it'll have to go.'

Dana shrugged and looked him straight in the eye. 'I know you don't live here, so it's really none of your business.'

He looked stunned for a moment, his eyes widening.

She smiled the smallest of smiles. 'Oh, I'll just bet you're surprised. Not like me to stand my ground, is it?' She took a breath. 'I've tried to be as nice as possible to you since we split up, for Jess's sake. I've bent over backwards to make sure your daughter never saw all the times you let her down, or were too busy, or just didn't think about her. But you suck as a father almost as much as you sucked as a husband, and there's not a thing I can do about that. Believe me, I've tried. It's just not in you, and I guess that's not your fault.'

After a moment's thought Jim narrowed his eyes and

stepped closer to hiss down at her. 'Maybe I'd have been a better husband if you'd been a better wife.'

He was trying to turn it onto her shoulders? Dana was stunned by his words. Not stunned by his predictability in arguing, but stunned by the person he'd become. When had he changed into the kind of man she wouldn't have spent five minutes with? Had she been so desperate to marry and settle down that she'd been blind to it all that time? Or had all the years of bickering changed him? They had changed her, from someone who lived life to the full into someone who never, ever took a chance. All the bickering had done to her really, in the end, was make her tired. Exhausted, in fact. But not so tired she couldn't fight her corner.

'You have no right to say that. You know it's not true. I tried long after you'd already made the decision to quit on our marriage and your daughter.'

'Maybe I'd have stayed interested longer if you'd not been so obsessed with having another baby. It was all you ever bloody thought about, wasn't it? If you'd just tried harder to be a wife you might have saved our marriage.'

She blinked. Her reaction time was down. She was exhausted, all right. Years of exhaustion were catching up on her. She even felt vaguely feverish, if truth be told. But as she'd spent all morning tidying the house, preparing food, and worrying over Adam's big surprise it was no wonder she was feverish.

Her words were low. 'No, and that shows exactly how much you know. I tried hard to be a good wife, a patient wife and a brave wife. All I ever did was try for the family I wanted us to be, and cry for the babies I lost. I guess I just chose to have a family with the wrong man.'

'Oh, and I suppose this time you think you have the right one?'

She looked him straight in the eye. 'Yes, actually, I think I do.'

'That's good to hear.'

She turned so suddenly she actually hurt her neck, and had to lift a hand to rub at it as she looked up into green eyes. Her eyes widened in surprise. 'How long have you been there?'

Adam smiled, his eyes soft and warm. 'Since you said the dog could stay.'

'Eavesdroppers never hear any good.'

'You know, I used to believe that.' Walking across to stand by her, he reached out and tangled his fingers with hers, looking down into her eyes. 'Just so you know—I'm probably going to have to hit this guy.'

She watched as he jerked his head in Jim's direction, dislodging his fringe with the movement. 'He'd sue you.'

'It'd be worth it.'

Her eyes noticed the split at the edge of Adam's mouth. 'What happened to your lip?'

'This?' His free hand reached up to touch the knuckles to his mouth, then he shrugged. 'It's nothing. Jack hit me.'

'Oh.' Untangling her fingers from the longer fingers that held hers, Dana backed up a step to pull out a seat at the kitchen table.

'I take it I'm forgiven for the dog, then?'

Jim's voice interrupted. 'No. It has to go back.'

Adam kept his eyes focused on Dana, who in turn rolled her eyes. 'I believe you were already told that it's none of your business.'

Dana reached to the small of her back to rub back and forth.

Adam frowned. 'You okay?'

She nodded.

'Oh, quite the family unit, here, aren't we?' sniped Jim.

Adam hunched down to look closer at Dana's face. She was flushed. He reached out and laid his fingers across her forehead. And warm.

'Babe, are you sick?'

'I'm f—'

'Well, we'll just see how much of a family you've got when she loses that baby. Because she will, you know.'

Adam's face changed as he looked into Dana's weary eyes. 'One second.'

Dana watched as he stood, turned, and pushed Jim up against the wall. 'I'm not going to hit you right now, because it's your daughter's birthday and it would be tough explaining to her why her dad is leaving in an ambulance.'

'Adam—'

He ignored Dana's voice. 'I haven't the faintest idea why you feel the need to be this way. Maybe it's guilt at the fact you don't know your own daughter well enough to know what she'd like for her birthday. Maybe it's because you weren't there for your wife when she needed you. But whatever reason you think you have for speaking to her the way you do, you'd do best to forget it.'

'Adam…'

He moved his face closer. 'Because if you don't start treating Dana with a little more respect you'll have me to deal with.'

'Adam!' Her voice grew more insistent.

'And you wouldn't like that.'

*'Adam!'*

He turned and looked over his shoulder at Dana just as she tried to stand and doubled with a cramp. Her eyes met his with a look of complete panic, her voice dropping to a low gasp. 'Oh, God.'

\*     \*     \*

Practically the entire Lewis family went to the hospital with them—a flotilla of cars making their way to the other side of town. Only Rachel stayed, to look after the children and Jess.

In the large waiting area Adam paced. He couldn't think what else to do. It was nearly an hour before a doctor appeared to talk to them. An hour in which he made some major decisions and finally found the bottle to inform everyone in the waiting room of what those decisions were.

Now the Lewis team was on *his* side.

Dana's eyes opened slowly, taking time to adjust to the light. Strong fingers squeezed hers and she looked into Adam's face. Her throat closed over. Oh, no. God, no.

'Hey.' He smiled at her.

She managed to swallow and waited for his words.

Getting up from the plastic seat, he sat on the edge of the bed beside her. His eyes widened slightly as a tear ran from the edge of her eye and into the pillow. 'Hey, what's that for?'

'I'm sorry.' She managed to whisper the words.

'What for? For getting sick? That's hardly your fault.' He reached a hand out and wiped away another tear. 'Don't cry. I've not mentioned it so far, but men hate it when women do that.'

With a shake of her head she managed to force out the words he hadn't said. 'I'm sorry I lost our baby. I did too much today. It's my fault.'

Adam frowned down at her, then freed both his hands to pull her up into his arms. Rocking her gently, he kissed her hair and whispered in a choked voice, 'You didn't.'

She pulled back from him until she could see his face. 'I didn't?'

'No.' He smiled. 'You have a kidney infection.'

'A kidney infection?'

His eyes sparkled. 'Have you noticed an echo in here?'

She stared at him, then blinked her tears away for a moment. 'Try not being funny for two seconds, could you?'

'I'm sorry. It's what I do in times of crisis.' He squeezed his arms a little tighter around her. 'Or when I've just had the life scared clean out of me by the woman I love.'

She searched his eyes as she asked the question. 'I didn't lose our baby?'

'No, you didn't.' He smiled again. 'And can I just mention how much I love the fact that you're now referring to the baby as *our* baby instead of *the* baby?'

A smile began to blossom somewhere inside her. 'I didn't lose our baby? I'm still pregnant?'

'Yep. You have one hell of a kidney infection, though. Temperature, lower back pain, cramps—the lot. But the doc says you'll live, and has given you antibiotics.'

'Antibiotics?' Her eyes grew concerned again.

Adam nodded. 'Yep, and I asked—and they're safe.'

Finally she managed a smile. Which promoted itself to a grin. Then something else hit her mind and she frowned. 'What did you say just then?'

'The antibiotics are safe for the baby. I knew you'd want to know that.'

She shook her head. 'Before that.'

'Which part?' His eyebrows raised in question.

'The scared bit.'

'Oh, *that* bit.' He shook his head, a serious expression on his face. 'I guess I could have picked a better time for that confession, couldn't I?'

She blinked up at him. 'You said "the woman I love".'

'I did, didn't I?'

Dana nodded.

He waited several long seconds, his face completely deadpan, and then said, 'You do know you're going to have to marry me now that you've got me?'

She stared at him.

It was Adam's turn to nod. 'I'm afraid so.'

'I'm not marrying you because of our baby, Adam.'

'No,' he agreed. 'You're marrying me because I'm in love with you.'

She frowned. 'No, you're not.'

'Yes, I am.'

She struggled back a little in his arms. 'No, you're not. You just think you are—because we're having a baby together and we just had the fright of our lives because we thought we'd lost it.'

'But we didn't.'

She stared at him incredulously. He couldn't know what he was saying. She searched his face for signs of deception—a hint that he wasn't completely convinced of what he was saying. But all she could see was warmth and sincerity and...something else...

She shook her head, her hair falling all around her shoulders. 'No, if we'd lost this baby you wouldn't be saying this right now.'

'You're right. I wouldn't.'

Her heart plummeted, despite the fact that she'd asked for the confirmation. 'You *don't* love me, Adam.' Her eyes dropped.

Adam took a deep breath and looked upwards for a second before looking back at her. 'Yeah, I do. But I wouldn't have been talking about getting married right here and now if we'd just lost our baby. I wouldn't have been able to talk.' He leaned closer, his voice a soft whisper. 'It would have hurt too much to talk.'

She felt her eyes filling again as she looked back up at his ridiculously handsome face.

His voice stayed low and hypnotic. 'Don't you cry on me again.'

She sniffed. 'I'm not.'

'Good.' He pulled her back against his chest, one hand smoothing the long dark hair against her back. Waiting until she'd relaxed against him, he continued, 'If we *had* lost this baby, Dana, I'd have wanted another one with you.'

She felt the tears come regardless. But she was hidden against his chest, his steady heartbeat against her ear, and she knew at least he couldn't see them.

His voice rumbled in his chest as he spoke again, sounding in stereo to her ears. 'I want dozens of babies with you after this one.'

She sniffed as quietly as she could manage.

His hand stilled on her hair and he glanced down at her head. 'You'd better not be crying down there.'

'I'm not.' Her voice was muffled. 'I'm listening.'

He glanced down again. 'That's a first.'

'You were at "dozens of babies".'

'I was, wasn't I?' He took a breath. 'You sneaked up on me, I think. Though I have to admit, since I'm on a roll here, that you're probably the reason I started my whole bachelor binge in the first place.'

She lifted her head to look up at him. 'What?'

A flush touched his cheeks. 'I think I fell a little in love the first time I met you. I couldn't take my eyes off you. Even bugged the hell out of Jack for an introduction. But then you treated me like a dose of lice.'

It was Dana's turn to blush.

'So I decided that I'd forget all about this haunting creature by playing the bachelor far and wide.' He shrugged. 'And I discovered I was good at it. No attachments. No heavy involvement. Until you came to work at the office. I guess eventually something had to give.'

'So you reckon you're in love with me?'

He nodded. 'Yes, I am.'

'And you're quite sure about that?'

Without further words he leaned down and brushed his mouth against hers, grimacing slightly at his split lip but then deciding it was worth the pain. He raised his head, his eyes inches from hers. 'Listen carefully, babe. I love you. You can argue with me 'til our fiftieth anniversary, if you like, but you're stuck with me. Haven't I been telling you that for weeks?'

'Yes, you have. But I thought it was because of—'

'I know you did. And at the start maybe I even convinced myself it was that too. But then I spent time with you, with Jess. And I realised I was right where I wanted to be. You're my family now.' He kissed her again. 'Marry me.'

'I have a really bad record with being married.'

'Only because you married the wrong guy.' He kissed her again. 'Marry *me*.'

'You think I'm anally retentive and a control freak.'

A shrug. 'You are. But I love you regardless. And anyway, I figure I'll balance that out.' Another kiss. 'So marry me.'

'You want to take on me and all my insecurities, a new baby, an eleven-year-old daughter and a dog? Become a family man?'

'Yes, yes, yes…' He looked up and thought for a second, kissing her quickly again as he counted. 'Technically the dog was already my idea, and, yes, absolutely I do. Just say you'll marry me.'

She waited for his eyes to meet hers again before smiling at him. 'What if I don't love you?'

'Then I'll have to spend every day convincing you that I'm the guy for you. It's what I've been trying to do for ages now. I'm a pretty great guy. My mother tells me so all the time.'

Laughter bubbled free out of her chest. 'I'll just bet. No bias there. And despite the chance that your head might swell up even more...' Her eyes softened. 'I have to say she might just be right.'

'You think so?' He smiled back at her. 'Then how can you *not* want to marry me?'

'We'll argue.' But she knew it wouldn't be in the same way she'd argued with Jim.

'I know.' He smiled contentedly.

She waited, smiling back at the silent determination in his eyes. 'But I'll love you for the rest of my life, Adam, I really will. I've never felt like this before. And it started for me a long time ago too, or I guess I would never have ended up pregnant in the first place.'

They smiled at each other as hospital noises continued outside her room. Then Adam leaned down again and they kissed until he couldn't take the pain in his lip any more.

Raising his head, he frowned and pressed his thumb against it.

Dana kissed his cheek, and touched the edge of the split in his lip with her fingers, her love finally allowed to shine from her eyes. 'Poor baby. How can I make that better for you?'

He grinned, laughed at the pain it caused, and hugged her tight. 'You could just damn well marry me.'

'Well, if you insist...' She leaned her cheek against the

vague stubble on his face to whisper in his ear, 'Though you could have asked me sooner and I'd probably still have said yes. With a little persuasion.'

He leaned back a little to scowl down at her with a spark of amusement in his eyes. 'I swear, woman, if you've just done that devious thing of yours on me…'

# EPILOGUE

'IT's a girl.'

There was a chorus of congratulations and grins as one by one the extended Lewis family stepped forward to engulf him in a hug.

'And Mummy?' Tess was the first to ask as she stepped into the circle.

He smiled. 'Exhausted, but fine. She says if I even think of touching her again until we find out what caused this one I'm a dead man, but apart from that…'

'She'll change her mind. You just wait and see.'

Adam grinned at his friend as he slapped him on the back. 'Yeah, she will. After all, who could resist?'

'You next, old pal,' Jack poked him in the stomach with a broad grin.

Adam nodded as Dana ambled up to his side, lifting his arm to let her body in close to his. 'Yep—can't wait.'

Dana snorted. 'Yeah, *he* can't wait. *I* know what's coming.'

'And the drugs are already on order, babe.'

'I've ordered a bucketload.' She stretched up to kiss her brother on the cheek. 'Congrats, Jack. We're all so pleased for you both.'

Jack nodded, leaning down to whisper in her ear, 'We all got there in the end, didn't we?'

Her eyes welled up. 'Yes, we did.'

'Whoa—no making my wife cry, you. I spend all day doing my best to make sure that doesn't happen.' Adam grasped Dana's hand and tugged her back a step. 'Is the baby in the nursery, then?'

Jack nodded, exhaustion showing on his happy face. 'Yeah, they took her down to let Tara get some sleep. I'm just going to look in on her again before I get some sleep myself.'

As the others closed in to have their say, Adam tugged Dana's hand and led her down the corridor until they got to the large windows of the nursery. The tiny country hospital had only a small nursery, with two occupants, so it wasn't hard to find the pink blanket covering their new niece.

Dana laughed at his enthusiasm to be the first to see her. He really had become quite the babyholic, grinning inanely at anything in a pram. He was looking forward to fatherhood with more excitement than she would ever have thought possible. It was funny, amazing, wonderful. She loved him for it.

'Look.' He whispered down into Dana's ear. 'She's tiny.'

'That's the size they come in, thank God.' She grinned up at him as he stepped behind her to encircle her, his hands coming to rest on the swell of her stomach. 'And that size is painful enough. Just keep thinking beach ball into golf ball hole.'

He laughed and kissed the top of her head, his hands moving in slow circles. 'Worth it, though.'

'Yes, it is.' Her hands rested on his and she caught sight of their reflection in the glass. They looked happy. She smiled. Maybe just because they were. With Adam she'd found the missing part of the puzzle—even if they had done things a little back to front.

She looked down at where their hands rested on their own baby. It wouldn't be long now before they'd be in a hospital like this one. Having passed what had always been the danger zone for her in the past, each day brought her a little more faith in the fact that it was going to happen. They were having a baby.

'What?'

'She glanced up at his face in reflection. 'What, what?'

'You're thinking something.'

'I'm constantly thinking something. I'm a highly intelligent woman.'

Adam smiled. 'I know, that's why you married me.'

Turning around, she linked her hands behind his neck and leaned back against the band of his arms. 'Yes, I did, didn't I?'

'Technically, we're still newlyweds.' He grinned down at her with all his patented Donovan charm on display. Technically, he was right—with them only being married six weeks. 'So *technically* we should still be—you know—*indoors*.'

'Helping find out what caused Jack and Tara's baby, you mean?'

'Yes, that's exactly what I mean.' He nodded enthusiastically, dislodging his fringe.

'So you want to go home, then?'

'Yes, Mrs Donovan, I most definitely do.' He leaned down to kiss her soundly. 'I'm homesick.'

They'd moved the day before to a huge house halfway between Jack and Tara's and the office, and it was home now. *Their* home. Dana blinked as she fought back a threatened wave of tears. Hormones still—because she certainly wasn't sad any more. Quite the opposite. She glanced down.

'Aw, hell, are you crying again?'

She shook her head. 'No.'

'Liar.'

She looked up with a smile. 'I can't help it if I'm happy. It's your fault. So you can just suck it up and get used to a few tears here and there.'

'Just so long as you don't blub for the next forty years.'

'I won't.'

He smiled at her with a now familiar warmth in his eyes. 'I love you, you know. Even if you are such a girl sometimes.'

Dana took a deep breath. 'And I love you. You've made my life what I always wanted it to be.'

'Even if we did things a bit out of order?'

She smiled at the questioning spark in his green eyes. The *All Things Good* list was really miles long now. 'Just so long as we got here in the end, I don't think it matters.'

'I agree.'

Their eyes widened at the statement they had once never thought to hear aloud. They laughed simultaneously, then kissed. Then Adam took her hand in his and led her towards the doorway, towards the car, towards home.

He grinned. The trap felt pretty damn good after it had closed.

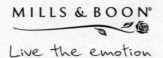

MILLS & BOON®

*Live the emotion*

# Virgin Brides

In March 2005 By Request brings
back three favourite novels by our
bestselling Mills & Boon authors:

The Virgin Bride *by Miranda Lee*
One Bridegroom Required!
*by Sharon Kendrick*
No Holding Back *by Kate Walker*

**These brides have kept their
innocence for their perfect
husbands-to-be…**

**On sale 4th March 2005**

0205/05

# FREE

## 4 BOOKS AND A SURPRISE GIFT!

We would like to take this opportunity to thank you for reading this Mills & Boon® book by offering you the chance to take FOUR more specially selected titles from the Tender Romance™ series absolutely FREE! We're also making this offer to introduce you to the benefits of the Reader Service™—

- ★ **FREE home delivery**
- ★ **FREE gifts and competitions**
- ★ **FREE monthly Newsletter**
- ★ **Books available before they're in the shops**
- ★ **Exclusive Reader Service offers**

Accepting these FREE books and gift places you under no obligation to buy; you may cancel at any time, even after receiving your free shipment. Simply complete your details below and return the entire page to the address below. You don't even need a stamp!

**YES!** Please send me 4 free Tender Romance books and a surprise gift. I understand that unless you hear from me, I will receive 6 superb new titles every month for just £2.69 each, postage and packing free. I am under no obligation to purchase any books and may cancel my subscription at any time. The free books and gift will be mine to keep in any case.

N5ZEE

Ms/Mrs/Miss/Mr...................................Initials ..........................
BLOCK CAPITALS PLEASE

Surname ....................................................................................

Address ....................................................................................

....................................................................................

..............................................Postcode ..........................

Send this whole page to:

The Reader Service, FREEPOST CN81, Croydon, CR9 3WZ

Offer valid in UK only and is not available to current Reader Service™ subscribers to this series. Overseas and Eire please write for details. We reserve the right to refuse an application and applicants must be aged 18 years or over. Only one application per household. Terms and prices subject to change without notice. Offer expires 31st May 2005. As a result of this application, you may receive offers from Harlequin Mills & Boon and other carefully selected companies. If you would prefer not to share in this opportunity please write to The Data Manager at PO Box 676, Richmond, TW9 1WU.

Mills & Boon® is a registered trademark owned by Harlequin Mills & Boon Limited.
Tender Romance™ is being used as a trademark. The Reader Service™ is being used as a trademark.

# WIN a romantic weekend in PARiS

*To celebrate Valentine's Day we are offering you the chance to WIN one of 3 romantic weekend breaks to Paris.*

Imagine you're in Paris; strolling down the Champs Elysées, pottering through the Latin Quarter or taking an evening cruise down the Seine. Whatever your mood, Paris has something to offer everyone.

For your chance to make this dream a reality simply enter this prize draw by filling in the entry form below:

Name _____

Address _____

_____Tel no: _____

**Closing date for entries is 30th June 2005**

Please send your entry to:

**Valentine's Day Prize Draw**
**PO Box 676, Richmond, Surrey, TW9 1WU**